I0552101

HAZY VIEWS
THE PREQUEL TO MURKY
WATERS RISING

Vanity Smith

DEDICATION

This book is dedicated to all of my sisters in arms. Stay focused. Continue to be great! Speak up and Stand out!

AUTHOR'S NOTE

Dear reader,

Welcome to the Murky Waters Series. For those of you who have read my previous book, thank you. For those of you just catching up, here is some helpful information.

This is a prequel, meaning it takes place before the first book in the series, Murky Waters. That said, the main characters of the series are Lace, Nika, Jen, and Sasha—you will learn all about them in detail in book one. So, do yourself a favor and read book one first.

I dug deep to write this prequel. Though this book is fiction, many of the stories of sexual harassment, sexual assault, domestic violence, and betrayal, though enhanced, are true. I have either personally experienced them or been there to wipe the tears from my sisters-in-arms' faces when they have. I write what I know, but, of course, with a creative, enhanced twist.

Thank you to my support team for their encouragement and inspiration throughout the process. I could not do this without your consistent willingness to listen and engage. You all are the real MVPs.

Thank you to my management team at work for hosting daily and hourly meetings that provided the reminder I desperately needed to keep writing so I could quit my job.

Do you want to help me quit my job? follow my writing journey on social media @VanitySmith.

Got a story you want to share with the world, but do not want to tell it yourself? Send it my way Vanity@vanitysmith.com, and I'll do my best to incorporate it into one of the upcoming books within the series.

Current books in this series:

Murky Waters Rising – Book 1

Hazy Views, the Prequel to Murky Waters Rising– Book 2

Thanks,

Vanity

CHAPTER 1
MRS.THOMPSON

Sally and Bill began discussing retirement when their youngest son entered high school. It had become a daily conversation once he graduated.

I always thought it was just talk, but they fooled me and finally made good on their promise to move south. We had been neighbors for just under 30 years. Jim and I bought this house just a month after Sally and Bill moved in. Sally was so welcoming. She made me feel at home in the neighborhood immediately, probably because she was new to the area herself. We clicked instantly. We talked for over an hour during our first meeting, and I knew at that moment we would be friends for life.

I had been married for a little under a year, and Sally had been married a little over four years when we met. She helped me through many trying marital times.

Marriage is great, of course, but no one tells you the real deal about marriage before you jump the broom. A lot of the lessons you learn on your own through trials and tribulations, and in marriage, they're plentiful.

Jim was my high school sweetheart, and he joined the Navy right after graduation. I was devastated when I found out. I thought that was the end of us. To my surprise, he proposed a week before he left for boot camp, and we were married a few days before he shipped out. Jim received his orders to Maryland right after boot camp and moved me up from South Carolina. It was my first time ever living without my parents and my first time living with a man. There were a lot of changes I was not prepared for, but Sally helped me navigate the waters of marriage. I like to think I helped her through some tough times, too.

Sally and I were always there for each other. I was there with her and in the delivery room with all her four babies. Sally was with me with all three of my babies as well. Sally and Bill were also there when we buried our middle daughter, Antoinette. Antoinette was murdered. Her life was stolen from her by a vicious animal. After that day, the sun never did shine as bright. She was 19 when we buried her. And Sally was by my side the entire time. Sally even took two months off work to stay by my side. There is no pain like losing a child.

Sally and I did everything together. We would sit on the porch and talk most days after work. Mostly, we gossiped about the other neighbors. I missed Sally, and I was extremely sad to be without her to talk to every day.

I was even sadder when my new neighbor, Lace, moved in. Lace was a young single mother with a little boy. She was nothing like Sally. Sally and I were close in age and shared a lot of the same likes and dislikes. We grew up in the same hometown of Greenville, South Carolina, too, but had not known each other until we became neighbors.

I wish Sally were here to meet this little heifer, Lace. I did not care for Lace myself. Jimmie thought I was not giving Lace a fair shake, but from what I could see, she is immature, inconsiderate, and selfish. She appeared to be an attentive mother, but she partied as if her life depended on it. She had different men coming over at all times of the evening, and that is a bad look for a single mother. Knowing all this, I was still drawn to get to know Lace. There is a tiny part of Lace that reminded me of Antoinette.

I tried being neighborly to Lace and would casually bring up her promiscuous behavior and how inappropriate it was, but the little hussy never wanted to hear it. We were at odds over a parking space. Lace was so mad I would park in her parking spot; she waved me off as often as she could. Not that my talking to her would have mattered, I doubt she would have paid me any mind. She was so insistent about parking in my spot that she would not hear anything else I had to say.

I had been parking in this spot for over 20 years. Sally and I never fought over parking. Although Sally did not drive, she and Bill had two parking spots deeded to them when they purchased their house. We only had one. Bill had his parking spot, and they allowed me to use the extra one when Jim and I bought a second car. If Sally and Bill had visitors, Bill had no problem parking in the circle where the visitors parked.

Lace did not care about any of that; all she cared about was that it was one of her two designated parking spots. I knew she only cared about the parking spot because she wanted her evening visitors to have easy access, but I didn't care for all the company she kept. If it were up to me, I'd make the parking situation as difficult as possible in hopes of keeping them away.

LACE

I graduated from my entry-level training course in November 2001 and received orders to Maryland. I was so disappointed. I called Mom, bawling my eyes out. My mother couldn't understand why. I didn't bother filling her in. I didn't want her to worry about me, but I should have thought about that before I called her. Mom met me in Pensacola with T and rode with me to Maryland to help me get settled in. Although I was technically homeless, Mom wanted to be there to help me find my first house. I decided a while back that I would purchase a home in every state I moved to, and although I hadn't done it in Virginia, I was determined to do it in Maryland.

I figured I would want to live somewhere close to the base. Meanwhile, we stayed in temporary housing on Fort Meade's base while I searched for my new home. Temporary housing was typically available for only 30 days or so. I knew for sure I wouldn't be able to find anything quickly, but I also didn't want to rent anything. That's how I got stuck renting in VA. I got comfortable staying in the same apartment complex with my coworkers and friends. It made life so easy. I had a bigger plan, though, and I didn't want to fall back into the same trap.

House hunting leave was granted after I checked into my command, and I dedicated all my off time to finding my first home. I searched the neighborhoods near Ft. Meade. I didn't know anything about Maryland or Ft. Meade, for that matter, but my sponsor showed me around and told me about the up-and-coming neighborhoods. My sponsor also introduced me to his friend, who was a realtor and an active-duty sergeant in the Army, Sergeant Hendricks.

Most of the up-and-coming neighborhoods were out of my price range, but there were a few neighborhoods with older single-family homes and townhomes that I could afford to live in. I had missed the real estate boom for the year. Most of the homes on the market were under contract or had recently sold, which meant the pickings were slim, to say the least. Sargent Hendricks worked with me diligently to help me find what I was looking for.

He would email me homes throughout the day, and my mother and I would scope out the neighborhood and decide if I wanted to see the property or not. We must have looked at over 30 homes. I was so picky. My mother, frustrated as I was, finally said "just pick a damn house. It's not your forever home, Lacey! If you would rent it, buy it. It's that simple. You're only going to be here a few years. It doesn't have to be perfect," she concluded.

Mom was right. I was putting too much emphasis on the perfect home. It was a few days later when I finally found a townhouse in a neighborhood where I could see myself living. It was in the Spring Meadows neighborhood of Severn, MD, not too far from the base. There were a lot of kids out when we went to tour the home. It seemed like a great community for kids, and the neighbors appeared friendly.

The townhouse did not check all the boxes for me, but it was good enough since it was just T and me. I wanted a home with a master bath, since I planned to do a lot of entertaining to get over Marcus, but that wasn't what I found. The townhouse was small, but enough.

The home had previously had only one owner, and it showed. They hadn't done any updates. Everything was in its original form. I would have to spend a significant portion of my bonus on fixing the place up. And I did just that. My townhouse had three bedrooms and one bath on the top level. A bathroom is located on the main level and another in the basement.

I closed on the house the week of Christmas. Mom stayed for the holiday and left shortly after. Sargent Hendricks helped me find a few contractors that he had worked with in the past to do some of the work. My first major projects were the kitchen and bathrooms on the top and main floors. They were so dated. The basement was partially finished and needed to be completed, but I decided to live with it for the time being.

Carlos, Sergeant Hendricks, that is, and I became good friends. He would come over often and make sure the contractors were on schedule and doing what they were supposed to be doing. The contractors were terrific and worked to finish my projects quickly. I'm sure it was due to their relationship with Carlos. Carlos had a way with people. I was drawn to him as a friend, though. We hung out after work, too. He had a thing for me, I knew it, but I wasn't interested in him in that way. I was still in love with Marcus and wasn't interested in any love interest. I needed to move on from Marcus and heal. I couldn't engage in relationship-type of shit with Carlos and get over Marcus. It would be too complicated.

Not that Carlos was my type. He was light-skinned and about the same height as me. There was nothing noticeable about Carlos. Once I got to know him, I saw that he was hilarious and very attentive. Still, I wasn't interested. Carlos didn't particularly like that, especially considering he knew I engaged in my fair share of random fuck encounters with other men. Some of which he knew.

I was at a Joint Duty command, so I had my pick of Army, Navy, Marine, and Air Force men. I was in "get over that nigga" heaven.

MRS. THOMPSON

Lace had been living here for almost five months, and we were finally becoming neighborly. Well, not really, but she wasn't rolling her eyes every time she saw me, and she started allowing young T to play with our grandkids when they visited. Lace also stopped fighting me over her parking spot and finally gave in on that battle. I thought that was a win. I think she only gave in because I checked on her while she was sick.

This generation doesn't know anything about being neighborly. "That's what neighbors do," I explained to Lace when she thanked me repeatedly for looking after T while she fought off the flu. She had a nasty bug, and the poor child was trying to battle it alone and still care for her son. Yep, it took a few months, but our relationship was flourishing. She would never be Sally, but she'd do.

Hubby and I fell in love with young T, and we loved having him around. We often asked for him even when the grandkids were not around, which was quite frequently. We truly enjoyed hearing his little feet walk around the house. He reminded us so much of our kids when they were young, now grown with children of their own, who had since all moved away. I believe if Antoinette were still alive, I would have one grandchild close to me. I imagine it would be a boy, and he would be much like T.

Hubby just adored young T. Hubby would often take T out into the yard, working with him on yard work. I made cookies almost every day for him. Lace would yell about it, but I ignored her. On days when Lace worked late, we would care for him in her absence. Although hubby and

I both knew "worked late" meant a happy hour, we didn't mind. T was a welcome distraction from our everyday lives.

Lace reminded me of Antoinette. They shared many of the same similarities and mannerisms. They both joined the Navy as well. Antoinette joined right out of high school, and I think Lace said she joined two years after high school. I wish they could have met. They might have been best friends.

I think that's why it was so vital for me to have a relationship with Lace. From the moment I saw her, I knew I wanted to know her, but she was just so damn self-absorbed, or so I assumed. The way Lace interacted with her mom and her son had Antoinette written all over it. I imagined that's how Antoinette and I would have interacted.

I thought of Antoinette frequently when I spoke to Lace, and that made me smile often. Nights like this, I missed Antoinette the most. We had grown so accustomed to our routine with T that it felt odd when Lace would change plans. "If he were Antoinette's son, our Thursday night sleepover would be permanent," I thought silently. Hubby and I didn't know what to do with ourselves on Thursdays anymore without T sleeping over. The nights seemed longer without him. It's funny how quickly one could fall into a routine. Hubby and I ate dinner, watched a little TV, and then I called it a night while hubby stayed up watching TV.

I stopped setting my alarm for Fridays once T started spending the night. He had a natural alarm clock and made sure everyone was up and ready to go so he wouldn't be late for school. T went to home care provided by someone who was once a principal at a private school. She was very punctual and taught the kids the importance of being on time, reminding them daily, "In your seat and ready to learn by 8:15 a.m. every weekday."

Naturally, without my alarm being set and no T to wake me, I had gotten a late start this morning. As I rushed to the car, I noticed Lace's truck was still parked in its spot, which was odd since it was well after 9:00 a.m. Lace did not mention having the day off, I thought. I took note of the truck and headed for work. I could not get Lace off my mind, though. "Something is off," I thought as I sat in traffic, which has been horrible since 911 happened.

A fifteen-minute ride had turned into an hour and a half. By the time I finally got through the Ft. Meade Reese Rd gate, it was almost 11:00 a.m. I was scheduled to leave at noon for a doctor's appointment. I contemplated going into the office for an hour and decided not to. I called my boss and told him I was taking the day off.

I decided to go straight to my doctor's appointment, hoping they could see me early since I would arrive early. But something in my gut was urging me to go home and check on Lace. I did not want to follow my gut feeling since I was so close to the doctor's office, but life experience had taught me that I always need to follow my first instinct.

Lace's car was in the same spot it was in when I left. I parked next to her and got out of my car. I knocked on Lace's front door and didn't get an answer. I went next door to my house to grab Lace's spare key to let myself in. Lace was sitting in the corner of her sofa, balled up. It was the same way I found Lace a few months ago, but this time, she was not sick. She was hurt and hurt badly.

I walked to Lace while she sat balled up on the edge of the sofa, T clung to her side. I grabbed T, washed him up quickly, and took him next door to hubby to watch. I raced back to Lace and sat next to her on the sofa. Lace fell into my arms and cried: "He raped me! He raped me!" she shouted repeatedly. I held Lace tightly and cried with her. I was furious. I warned Lace about the company she kept, and now this has happened. However, it was not the time for I-told-you-so. I stayed silent and allowed Lace to just cry. I reached in my pocket for my phone to call the cops,

Lace looked up and grabbed the phone from me, "No cops!" she whispered through her tears.

I did not know what to do. I knew why Lace did not want the cops involved, but we needed to call someone. Lace was uninhibited and sexually free. She knew how she would be looked at and judged in the eyes of the law. I held Lace tightly for a long time before finally speaking, "We have to call someone, Lace!" Lace didn't move. With her head still buried in my chest, I heard her faint voice ask me to call Sasha.

I didn't have Sasha's number, so Lace dialed the number for me. Lace continued to cry as I held her. Sasha answered on the third ring, and I urged her Nika and Jen to get up to our house as soon as they could, providing no details at all. I didn't know if they would come, but I did tell her that Lace needed them.

There was no way Lace would be able to go through this alone. I wanted to call her mom, but she begged me not to.

When Lace finally stopped crying, I asked her if she knew who did this to her, she tried to tell me, but her lips quivered every time she tried to talk. I knew I should have called the cops, but I was torn.

Antoinette was raped while she served in the Navy, and she did everything right. She called the cops who escorted her to the hospital. The police called my hubby and me, and we met Antoinette at the hospital. My baby was beaten, crying, and shivering when I saw her. I went to grab her, to hold her, but a nurse of some sort pushed me away. "Ma'am, we need to examine her first!" the nurse said. I remember that day like it just happened.

I walked slowly behind Antoinette and the nurse into a cold all-white examination room. I wanted to hold her hand, but they would not even allow me to do that. Instead, I sat in a chair in the corner and watched with tears streaming down my face as they poked and prodded her. There were so many people in and out of the room. Medical and police staff took pictures of all her injuries. It was horrific, watching my daughter go through that.

Even more horrific than that was watching the way the military law enforcement agency handled the case. Antoinette stayed on a joint base, which meant the military had jurisdiction over all criminal cases that accrued on the base. She was blamed for her own rape. It was a military policeman, the Corporal's word against Antoinette's. She never stood a chance. "He didn't have a bruise on him," I was told. I never had the opportunity to see him. I had hoped to see him that night so I could lay hands on him, but he was protected.

The Corporal lied and said it was consensual, but it was not. If it was consensual, why was my daughter beaten within inches of her life?

Antoinette was a virgin and was saving herself for marriage. She would never have sex with someone who was just a friend. Her rapist befriended her under false pretense. Antoinette had something he wanted, and he did whatever he could to take it. He raped her, took her virginity, and left her there soaking in her own blood. Nothing ever happened to him either. He was never even arrested.

After the rape, Antoinette was teased and retaliated against, but she fought back. She told any and everybody that would listen that the Army allowed a rapist to continue to serve. Army leadership at the time wanted to silence Antoinette. She was threatened with being kicked out of the Navy if she did not stop making "false accusations." The good old boy network would do whatever it took to protect its own. That is how the military works. Military leaders who have the authority and opportunity to make a difference cannot care less about protecting the female Soldiers, Airmen, Sailors, and Marines.

I urged her to get out, practically begged. But she refused. She wanted justice and was determined to get it. Antoinette, however, finally agreed to move off the base. Within a month of her move, she was found murdered in her apartment. They transferred the Corporal that raped her immediately, following Antoinette's murder, but not before he was promoted. I wasn't about to let what happened to Antoinette happen to Lace. No way in hell!

CHAPTER 2
SASHA

The ride up to Lace's was uneasy. Nika and I talked the entire time, trying to fill the space, but Jen didn't have much to say. I knew her mind was all over the place. She and Robbie were no longer in love, but she felt that there should have been a level of respect that he had for her as the mother of their child. But Robbie was different. He did not respect himself. No way he could respect Jen. I could not imagine walking in on Carter fucking another bitch! I would kill them both.

"Why do you think it's so hard for Lace to get over Marcus?" Jen finally spoke. "I don't know," Nika responded. "Maybe she really loved him." We all laughed hysterically. Lace told us she had fallen in love with Marcus, but no one believed it. She had known him for only a few months. She had relationships with randoms that lasted years, and half of them, she couldn't remember their names. Jen continued to laugh. She laughed so long and so hard that her laughs turned to sobs. She was hurting. We knew there would be some tears along the way. Jen continued to cry most of the ride.

We had been taking this ride to Lace's, Maryland, so often that it was beginning to feel like a second home. We enjoyed spending time with Lace in her new home and exploring DC. It always felt like a mini-vacation, waiting to exhale. But lately, Nika, Jen, and I had been getting tired of the "woe is me, my heart is broken, Lace." It was quite over the top, especially for Lace.

Plus, we all had our own shit to deal with. I, for some reason was still struggling to get over my last miscarriage. I needed to discuss it with someone. Sometimes, I felt like I was in a state of depression, but I had decided not to tell the girls about it. I needed a professional, I thought.

Not that my friends would not be comforting, but I hate those pity eyes Jen, Nika, and Lace would give me when I told them my body betrayed me. Sometimes I thought it was a sign from God that I was not supposed to have any more kids, but Carter and I both wanted at least one more child, preferably a little girl.

We had been trying so hard before he left for his deployment, and I was thrilled when I got pregnant. I wanted to give my body a rest after the first miscarriage, but Carter was not having it. He thought the more we fucked, the better our chances were. Clearly, he was right, because I got pregnant again. However, that is not quite how the ovulation cycle works. I was certain it wasn't taught to men, though. I attempted to educate him once, but as soon as I started talking, I decided not to. His facial expression told me everything I needed to know—he would never understand. I chuckled at the thought of that.

Carter grew up an only child, and he hated every minute of it. He told me when we first met that he wanted a huge family, and I was willing to give him one. "We'll take as many children as the Lord is willing to bless us with," I had told him. Lately, it seemed as though God was only teasing me with the blessing.

We arrived at Lace's house in just under three hours. We hadn't had a chance to tell Lace about Jen walking in on Robbie since we hadn't spoken to her. Ms. Thompson called and instructed us to get to her house as quickly as possible. Although we were sick of Lace and Marcus, we wanted to be there for Lace in her time of need. Lace was always there for each of us, no matter what. So, we all gathered right after work, dropped the kids with Mrs. Rogers, Nika's mom, and headed up.

As soon as we parked, Lace's screen door flew open. Mrs. Thompson came rushing out. "Get in here, girls," I felt something drop in the pit of my stomach as Mrs. Thompson ushered us into the house. Something was wrong, terribly wrong.

When I entered the house, the first thing I noticed was dried blood in the hall leading to the living room where Lace sat on her oversized sectional, balled up in the corner. She was crying, which was unusual. Although she was still hurting over Marcus, she had not actually cried in quite some time.

"Lace," Nika spoke softly, "what's wrong?" Lace lifted her head, and I could not believe what I saw. I screamed a gut-wrenching scream, and tears began to flow as I became frozen where I stood.

NIKA

Clearly, this trip was not about Marcus. I felt so stupid. I was just in the car thinking on the way up there that this was my last visit to deal with Lace's Marcus shit. Now standing in front of my beaten and battered friend, I was horrified. We asked Lace what happened repeatedly, but she would not respond. Ms. Thompson stood there watching and waiting, but Lace wouldn't speak. "I found her like this," Mrs. Thompson said. T was here, I took him next door and tried to find out what happened. "Talk to us, Lace," Jen asked nicely. "Tell us what happened," she pleaded.

Lace was trying to speak, but each time she tried, her swollen lips quivered. Lace was beaten badly. Her eyes were swollen, and her lips were as fat as could be. She had bruises all over her body. There was dried blood on her face, hair, and thighs. Mrs. Thompson walked over and switched out the ice packet that sat next to Lace. As I watched Lace shiver and cry, I began to cry, realizing I could not help her. I did not know what to do. I sat on the floor, as close as I could, and held her hands. Jen walked over and sat next to her on the sofa. Sasha remained standing, frozen near the staircase as tears flowed down her face. We could not get anything out of Lace. "Are you in pain?" Jen asked, and Lace responded by nodding her head yes. Sasha, closest to the stairs, announced that she would go up to get some meds. I held Lace's hands tightly, comforting her as much as I could when I heard Sasha rush back down the stairs with no meds in hand. "Lace, please tell us what happened," Sasha asked frantically as tears continued to stream down her face. "Your bedroom is a mess, and there's blood all over the dresser and bed. Who did this? What happened?"

Mrs. Thompson finally broke the ice and filled us in on the details. Lace had not told her who did it, so we all assumed it was a random. "How long have you been sitting here, Lace? We need to call the cops," I said before getting a response to my previous question. Lace looked at Mrs. Thompson for what looked like approval, and finally, words came out of her mouth. "I am not calling the cops. I am going to kill him myself," Lace announced. "Will you help me?" she asked.

I looked at Lace, and I knew she was hurt and upset, and she might change her mind in the morning, but I thought fuck that! "Let's do it and if you change your mind tomorrow, then we don't have to," I said, rubbing Lace's hand. "What the fuck is wrong with you, Nika?" Sasha screamed. "Lace is just upset right now, she doesn't mean what she's saying," Sasha continued while Jen cut her off and announced, "I am in... Fuck these niggas. Why? Why do they get to treat us like this? They can't anymore. How dare he, how dare he treat my friend like this? How dare he?" Jen continued to yell until her cries turned into sobs.

Emotions were flying high. Jay had been knocking me around for almost two years now. And I was already sick of it. I was nowhere near as strong as Lace, but if she needed my help to rid the world of this rapist son of a bitch, I would be there for her. I thought to myself that if I were able to kill this guy, then maybe one day I'd be strong enough to stop Jay from beating me.

We all stared at Sasha. She was pacing the floor. Sasha's life was perfect. She did not hate men the way I hated Jay or the way Jen hated men at that moment. That is why she could not agree. She was not angry enough.

"Look at our friend, Sasha. Look at her!" I yelled. Sasha stared long and hard through her tears at Lace while she continued to pace the floor. Mrs. Thompson's voice broke our silence as she began to tell us the story of her daughter, Antoinette. Mrs. Thompson was in tears as she shared with us her most painful memories. We all cried for her, even Sasha. Lace had never heard the story either. While Mrs. Thompson continued, Lace's face became bloodshot red when she heard the name, Hendricks. Lace started shaking and rocking hard back and forth as she screamed, "it was him. It was Sergeant Hendricks". Lace jumped off the sofa and hugged Mrs. Thompson tightly, and they both cried as their tears flowed. I cried for Mrs. Thompson. I could not imagine burying DD. The thought of it frightened me.

JEN

"Lace, are you saying the same guy that raped Mrs. Thompson's daughter is the guy that raped you?" I asked. Lace, through her swollen lips, spoke almost in a whisper. "It's the same name. I don't know. What are the odds?" Lace asked. Sasha listened intently through her tears. "If it's the same guy, I'm in," Sasha announced. "If it's not, I'm out," she continued. "What is the fucking difference? A rapist is a fucking rapist," I said in a heightened tone.

It did not matter to Sasha. She did not care. She was only in on the plan if we were killing a two-time rapist, not a one-time rapist. "That is fucking stupid. Does it really fucking matter? Clearly, guys with the last name Hendricks are all rapists. Fuck it! Let's line'em up and execute all the motherfuckers!" I exclaimed.

I did not say it to be funny, but Mrs. Thompson, Sasha, Nika, and I all laughed. We laughed so hard at the thought of lining up a group of men and killing them because of their last name. Amid our laughs, I looked over at Lace, and she was not laughing. She never even cracked a smile.

After our hardy laugh, I took Lace upstairs to help her get cleaned up. Sasha was right. Lace's room was a mess. I could see the imprint from where something had been smashed into the mirror. The sheets were off the bed as if she had been yanked while holding onto the edge of the bed. The lamp was knocked over, and the broken pieces were on the floor. There was a trail of blood leaving Lace's room, going down the stairs. The trail abruptly stopped at the third step. I wondered what happened: "Why did the trail suddenly stop?" Lace saw me staring. "You should see the other guy," she said as she broke out into tears.

"Why didn't you shoot him? Where is your gun, Lace?" I asked. "I couldn't get to it in time," Lace responded through quivering lips. I hugged my friend and helped her remove her robe. That was all she wore. I stared at Lace while I helped her get in the shower. He had done a number on her body. She had bruises everywhere. As I helped Lace shower, I pulled broken pieces of glass from her hair and skin. Lace cried the entire time. She was broken. I had never seen her like that before. I tried to be as strong as I could for her, but I was weak, and I too cried.

Lace and I didn't talk while I helped wash her up. Instead, my thoughts went to Robbie and what he had done. "Maybe what Robbie did wasn't so bad," I thought. "Do I really want to live a life like Lace's? Random men coming in and out of my life and bed; having to sleep with a gun under my pillow because you do not know what these random fuckers are capable of doing. Maybe I can forgive Robbie, he is the devil I know," I thought silently.

By the time we finished in the bathroom, Lace had stopped crying. "I'm tired," she whispered.

"I know. We are going to sleep downstairs if that is OK with you," I spoke softly. Lace didn't reply; she nodded her head in agreement instead. We walked slowly down the stairs. Sasha and Nika had just finished putting the final touches on the pull-out sofa bed. Lace lay down, and the three of us lay next to her. Mrs. Thompson sat on the other end of the sectional and kept watch until Lace fell asleep.

Once Lace was asleep, we got into action. Mrs. Thompson went next door to check up on T and her husband. Nika went upstairs and started cleaning Lace's room. I could hear Nika's cries as I cleaned the blood off the stairwell wall. There was so much blood. I did not think it was all Lace's, though. It had to be some of her attacker's blood. Lace was a fighter. She looked like shit, but I also knew she put up one helluva fight.

I wanted to know what had happened to Lace, but I had to realize that Lace would probably never tell us. We would probably never know. Sasha stayed on the bed, cuddling Lace, while she cried in her sleep. I felt helpless as I scrubbed the walls with a mixture of bleach and water. After I finished the walls, I started on the blood-stained carpet. Lace had a carpet cleaner and solution, but I wasn't sure if it was sufficient to clean up the mess. It seemed like the more I shampooed the carpet, the more blood appeared. At that point, I figured it had to be all in my head. I finished up what I could and put away all the cleaning supplies I used.

I went into the kitchen to pour a glass of wine. I could still hear Nika's sobs from upstairs and decided to pour her a glass, too. I walked up the steps to help Nika finish cleaning Lace's room. We drank our wine silently. Nika's face was swollen from crying. I hugged my friend. I knew that she experienced that life regularly. She did not share it with us, though. She protected Jay. She wanted us to think her marriage was perfect, but we all knew the truth. I did not know if Nika was crying for herself or Lace. We did what we could in Lace's room, showered, and headed back downstairs for the night. Lace and Sasha were fast asleep. We joined them on the pullout and were asleep within minutes.

Mrs. Thompson returned the next morning. She brought pictures of Antoinette at her best and her worst. I did not know why Mrs. Thompson kept those pictures, and I had prayed that she would not look at them often. Seeing the pictures of her daughter and the life she had reminded me of Lace a little. She was spunky, and her personality showed in every photo. We laughed as Mrs. Thompson shared stories about her daughter. And we cried when we heard that there was no action taken against the person who had viciously raped her on base. It angered me.

I, too, had been harassed and sexually abused in the Navy; I mean, we all had. I honestly did not know one female service member who had not been harassed or sexually assaulted. My first year in the Navy: I was working in the squadron's store, doing my ninety days of temporary duty. The job itself was cool. The people I worked with were even more amazing. The joy of the Navy was the people you met along the way and became friends with or family to. However, not everyone was worth keeping in your memory bank, though.

My supervisor at the time was a complete misogynistic asshole. He treated all women like second-class citizens. Actually, he treated women worse than second-class citizens. His name was AT1 Raymond. I would never forget him. Sadly, he had taken up space in my bank, but it is not a favorable memory. He was my first encounter with sexism, harassment, and sexual assault in the Navy, but throughout my four-year career, he was not my last.

AT1 Raymond was such a jerk. The squadron's store had six picnic tables and a TV. It was set up like a civilian break room. AT1 would walk in throughout the day, look around, and if only the females that worked there were present, he would throw one leg up on the table, put his hands down his pants, and scratch his balls right in front of us. He would get deep down in there and just go to town scratching. Then the fucking bastard would flick whatever came out toward us. He never did it when any of the guys were around, though. He had no respect for women, and everyone knew it. I was 100 percent positive he had raped a couple of women and gotten away with it. There were rumors around the command about him raping women. I was not sure if I totally believed it until I had my own very close encounter with him.

One morning, I was reading the LINK magazine in between serving my fellow sailors. AT1 came in screaming and yelling about something. I ignored him because he was always screaming about something. He had no idea how to use his inside voice. He was such an ass.

The next thing I heard from AT1 was, "Airman Adams, you ain't good for nothing but fucking and reproducing. Put that damn magazine down! You know damn well your mutt ass can't read." "Fucking cock sucker," I mumbled. He laughed as he yanked me by my hair and forced me to my knees. "I'll show you a fucking cock sucker," he said.

I was shocked and appalled as he pushed my head toward his dick. It was the middle of the fucking workday and this fucker had the gall to try and force me to suck his dick. Instincts kicked in, and I bit the shit out of him. He buckled, and I ran out and went to the closest office I could find, which happened to be the personnel man's shop. I was frantic and explained to the on-duty Chief what had happened. The Chief responded, "Now, surely, you have been handled like that before. Why make a big deal out of a little joke?" I had indeed been talked to crazily before and even engaged in rough sexual acts, but that was consensual, and this was not, and it was not okay. I reported both AT1 and the Chief on duty to the Command Master Chief and was told, "You must have misunderstood what he meant." And nothing happened. I reported it, and absolutely NOTHING happened. I could not believe it.

This was when it was zero tolerance for sexual harassment, but what "zero tolerance" really meant was, "Do not go to the media! Do not tell your family! Do not tell anyone outside of this command!" It was the good ole boy network protecting their own. AT1 was retiring in a few months, and they did not want one of his "jokes" to smudge his great reputation, I was told. Ridiculous!

It was almost expected to be sexually harassed and abused in the Navy, and have nothing happen to the abuser, but this was different. This was full-blown rape. This was past typical assault. The anger I felt just thinking about what Antoinette must have gone through and what Lace just went through made my stomach weak and intensified my desire for wanting to kill the bastard who did this to Lace.

CHAPTER 3
LACE

I was sitting on the couch listening to Mrs. Thompson. Well, not really listening, just staring, and I started speaking randomly before I even realized I was doing so. *"He did not break in. He had a key. We ate together. We worked out together. I thought he was my friend. Not just a typical friend, but one of my close friends. I told him everything. We hung out all the time. We talked every day about everything. He had watched my son for me. I had spent the night at his house. I trusted him."*

I continued to speak, although I am sure most of my words were unintelligible. The betrayal I felt intensified as I said every word. *"We had planned to dip out of work early to do some shopping for basement décor. So, yesterday morning, he picked me and T up, and we dropped T off at daycare. We went to work for a few hours, then dipped out around noon. We spent the rest of the day looking at countertops and tiles for the basement. We had a great day—laughing, talking, playing around, and just enjoying each other's company.*

After I decided on the countertops and tiles, we went to pick T up and then met up with some of his friends and had dinner. During dinner, I made plans to see one of my new randoms. He heard me and asked when I would give him a chance. I laughed and reminded him that we were just friends, and I wanted to keep things that way. "Our friendship is perfect. Sex would ruin the friendship and fuck things up," I said. He agreed. He was not even mad.

When we finished dinner, he brought us back home and told me he would see me later.

I put T to bed at 8:30 p.m., as I always do. I had an hour before my random showed up around 9:30 pm. When my random arrived, we talked, drank, laughed, and watched TV a little. Eventually, we started fooling around and then we fucked a couple of times. We drank throughout the night, and I was a little tipsy, but I did not think I was drunk.

After we finished our business, we chatted a little more. He tried to stay the night, but I was not having it. I should have let him, then this probably would not have happened. It was getting late, so we said our goodbyes, and I walked my random out around one in the morning. I locked both the top and bottom locks when he left. I made my way back upstairs, checked on T, showered, went to bed, and was asleep within minutes.

I do not know how long I was asleep before I heard someone coming into my bedroom. I originally thought it was T, but I heard the door close. When I looked up, I saw a shadowy figure. At first, I couldn't make out who it was, but as my eyes came into focus, I saw it was Carlos, and he was undressing. I screamed at him and asked him what the fuck he was doing in my house. By this time, he was completely naked, and he said it was his turn. I was so confused, dazed, and probably a little intoxicated. I yelled for Carlos to get the fuck out. I told him I had company on the way, and he would be here any moment. He told me I was a liar and that he watched my company leave, so he was not going anywhere. He said, "If you can fuck all those random niggas, you're going to fuck me, too." Carlos crawled on top of me and tried to force himself on me. I started fighting him off me and kneed him in the dick. He buckled over, and I stood up and tried to get to my closet, that's where I kept my gun now, and Carlos knew that. He was the one who recommended I put my gun up out of T's reach. Carlos grabbed me with one hand and threw me back on the bed. He started punching me while I was on the bed. I was punching him back, but he was stronger than I, and he had the advantage of being sober. I reached for my bedside lamp and hit him across the head. We both tumbled off the bed when the lamp landed on him. The lamp broke, and the glass went everywhere. I think that is where most of my cuts came from. I tried to run when we both hit the floor, but Carlos overpowered me again. He stood up right behind me and hurled me into the mirror on my dresser. He smashed my head into the mirror several times to subdue me before he began choking me. I tried fighting back as much as I could, but at some point, I must have passed out. When I came through, I was lying on the bed, and he was in me, stroking me, kissing me, and smiling. He kept saying, "Doesn't this feel good? Why did you fight me? Why did you make me do this to you?" I did not answer him, and I didn't cry. He had my hands pinned down, but my legs were free. I kept trying to fling him off me, using the strength in my legs but that infuriated him more and with his dick still in me, he punched me repeatedly with one hand while choking me with the other. The next thing I remembered was waking up, and he was sleeping next to me. The motherfucker had the audacity, the fucking balls to go to sleep. He was in good hearty sleep, too. I jumped up and ran to my closet to grab my gun. I must have moved too fast because he woke up and ran behind me. I could not reach the closet, so my next thought was to get out of the house. I ran out of the room, down two stairs, and leaped across the stairwell. Carlos followed suit and landed directly on top of me. When I awoke again, he was gone, and the door was locked. Both the bottom lock and the deadbolt. That was when I realized he must have made a copy of the key the contractors used to come in."

I did not look at anyone while I told them what happened. I looked down mostly. I was ashamed. I was hurt. I felt disgusted. I felt used. I felt betrayed. I felt powerless. No one said a word. They sat silently, looking and waiting. *"You know what else he said while he choked me on the bed, "Do not go running your mouth, Lace! No one will ever believe a whore like you. You are just another mattress for the men on base and off base, too, for that matter."* And then he laughed. Saying that out loud brought tears to my eyes, and I could not help but continue crying.

I did not want to cry anymore, though. I wanted to kill him badly. "He will never do this to another woman," I said while tears continued to fall. NEVER!!!

When I looked up, I noticed everyone in the room was crying. They were staring at me with pity in their eyes. Looking at me as if I were broken, damaged goods. I felt like broken, damaged goods, too. I had never felt such misery in my life. "Why would he do this to me?" I asked. It was rhetorical, and everyone must have known because no one offered up an answer. We sat there, all of us, in complete silence for what felt like a lifetime.

SASHA

We were completely engulfed, listening to Mrs. Thompson's story, when I heard Lace's voice. She spoke in almost a whisper. She recapped everything that happened the night before. There was not a dry eye in the room. While Lace spoke softly, I made up my mind that it did not matter who it was; if she wanted to kill him and needed my help to do it, then that's what we were going to do. It did not matter to me that I did not know the first thing about killing anyone. None of us knew anything, nor did we know where to start, but we were determined to figure it out.

When Lace finally finished telling us about her ordeal, I was enraged! The nerve, the boldness! I went to the kitchen and grabbed some paper towels. "Clean your face, Lace," I demanded. "There will be no more tears shed over this motherfucker; do you hear me? That goes for everyone!" I said, looking around the room. Everyone grabbed paper towels and cleaned their faces. When all the tears ceased, I asked: "What's the plan?"

No one said a fucking word. "Go figure!" Everyone wanted him dead, but no one knew how we would do it. There was complete silence for a long time before Lace finally spoke again.

"I want to torture him. I want to make him pay for what he did," Lace whispered.

"Lace, you said he knew where your gun was. Have you checked to see if it is still there?" Jen asked randomly.

Lace shook her head and immediately got up, walking upstairs. I followed closely behind her. You could see she was in pain. She walked hunched over with a limp. She really needed to go to the doctor, but had refused the offer several times. Once upstairs, she grabbed her step stool and checked the box where she had put her gun, and sure enough, it was gone. Carlos had taken the gun. Lace turned toward me as she walked back downstairs, looking completely deflated, defeated, and devastated.

"He planned this, probably, for months," I said once Lace confirmed her gun was missing.

"We need a plan, and we need to decide when this will happen," Jen said. "I want to do it today," Lace announced.

Mrs. Thompson chimed in, "Today is not a good day, Lace. You're not strong enough to do anything like that. You've got to be smart if this is really what you want to do."

"She's right, Lace. Let's get a plan together and then figure out a day and time." We talked the rest of Saturday and late into Sunday night. Again, neither of us had ever done anything like this and had no idea how we would manage to pull it off or how we would feel afterward. But we were determined to see it through. After hours of discussion, the plan was finalized. Nika, Jen, and I hugged our friend as tightly as we could and headed back to Virginia.

Nika drove, but I could tell something was bothering her. "You OK, Nika?" I asked. "Yeah, I am just focused on the drive. I want to make good timing," Nika responded. Jen looked at me through the rearview mirror as I sat in the back seat and rolled my eyes. Nika was lying, and we all knew it. She could not lie to save her life. She feared Jay. He probably had her on a curfew, and she missed it. So now she would have to deal with his bullshit when she got home.

I considered addressing it, but then opted not to. I had my own shit to deal with. I found out I was pregnant three weeks after Carter left on his deployment and miscarried shortly afterward. "I think I'm suffering from depression since my last miscarriage," I blurted out. I did not even know why I said it, but I did. Nika looked at me through the rearview mirror, her voice soft and sweet as could be, and said, "I'm so sorry, Sasha. I wish I could take that pain away from you. I know how badly you want another child."

Nika then pulled over, got out of the car, and opened the backseat car door. She motioned for me to get out of the car, and when I did, tears for my loss flowed. Nika held me tightly. Jen got out of the vehicle and came around and hugged me, too. We stood there on the side of the road, embraced and entangled in one another's arms until my tears stopped flowing.

Nika and Jen had both recently had abortions. They did not tell me. It was Lace that told me. She thought I knew already. I was so angry with them. Jen had an abortion because she was planning on getting out of the Navy soon, was in school full-time, and did not want the added responsibility. Nika had an abortion because she did not wish to have the devil's spawn child. She hated Jay. She tried to act as if she did not. Nika had a dumb ass fairytale idea about marriage how things were just supposed to be so perfect. That was not the case once she married Jay.

It is not the case in any marriage, but Nika lived in fantasy land. She was so judgmental about women who left their husbands. She would always make snide comments about how one must work hard to keep one's marriage together. "Anything worth having is worth fighting for," she would say. "I guess you feel that way when you're getting your ass beat on a regular," I thought to myself.

I was furious at them, but during our embrace, my anger subsided. I still felt some type of way as I was struggling to conceive and they are killing babies for selfish ass reasons. But it was no longer anger. It's amazing how calming a genuine embrace could be.

I got pregnant with our first child without even trying. I didn't know why this time was so much harder, but it was quite difficult. My mother thought it was the stress leading up to Carter's deployment, but I wasn't stressed then, and I still don't feel stressed now. "This is military life, and I have prepared for it, and things are great between Carter and me, even in his absence. We are as happy as any couple can be," I'd tell anyone.

The three of us drove back in silence after our stop on the side of the highway. Each immersed in her thoughts, I was sure. Nika stopped by her mom's so we could pick up the kids. She left DD with her mom. We dropped Nika off afterward.

"Look at his ole stupid ass," Jen snarled as we were pulling off from Nika's. I looked up and saw Jay fumbling with what looked like his dick in his hand. He was such an ass. I rolled my eyes and kept driving. Jen had already decided to stay the night by me. Which was cool. I wanted to be in the company of someone other than my son, Mason, and I thought I needed the noise. When we arrived at my house, Jen took the kids up and prepared them for bed.

They could have stayed up for all I cared, I had already decided I wasn't going to work the following day, so both could have stayed home with me. But Jen wanted some adult quiet time without thinking about Robbie or Sgt Hendricks. I agreed with her. So much had happened in a matter of just a few days. It was crushing.

I got a bottle of wine and poured us each a glass. By the time Jen came back down, I was deep into the corner of my sofa. Jen grabbed her wine and headed for the kitchen. I heard pots and pans rattling, as well as the fridge and counter doors opening and closing. I did not even bother to ask what she was doing.

When Jen was mad, happy, or sad, she would cook or bake. I was not sure what we were about to snack on, but I was ready for it. It's something about her cooking when she's emotional. It usually tasted like it was made with love, and I needed some love at that moment. Carter's deployment had been extended twice already, and I was missing him more and more as each day passed.

Jen was having the time of her life in the kitchen—cooking and crying—by the time she was done, I had almost finished the first bottle of wine. My laptop sat next to me on the sofa. After staring at it for far too long, I picked it up to check my email. I did not know why I bothered. Carter's messages were scarce, to say the least. I had been waiting two weeks already for an email letting me know when they would arrive home, but nothing had come. It had become discouraging to check my email. Even with the constant disappointment, I was still drawn to check it.

To my surprise, there was a message from Carter. I was so giddy and excited. I started smiling from ear to ear as I went to refill my wine glass, only to realize the bottle was empty. I ran into the kitchen to grab another bottle. Jen looked at me, puzzled, but continued doing what she was doing. I popped the cork on a fresh bottle, poured us another glass, and plopped down on the sofa.

Sailors were not allowed to give out their actual return dates or port dates when they were out to sea. So, they devised cryptic ways to inform their family of their whereabouts. I wanted to enjoy Carter's note and was hoping to get some good news finally. I opened Carter's email like a kid on Christmas morning, and it read, "I am in the mood for steak and potatoes. What do you think about having that for dinner on April 24?" I looked over at the calendar and saw that April 24 was just three weeks away.

I jumped for joy! The USS Vella Gulf was coming home! I started screaming and dancing like a little kid. Jen. came out of the kitchen and joined right in.

"What are we dancing about?" Jen asked through a wide smile.

"Carter will be home in three weeks," I yelled. We must have been dancing for a while, as I started to smell something delicious.

Jen walked out of the living room into the kitchen, and I followed closely behind. She had made brownies and a dozen oatmeal raisin cookies. We allowed them to cool as Jen and I sat, drank wine, and talked.

"Three weeks is perfect timing," Jen announced.

"How so?" I asked.

"We have to go up to Maryland the weekend prior for the show," Jen reminded me.

"The show" was code for killing Carlos Hendricks. We thought it would be odd to straight-up call it "killing", so we called it "the show". The show was scheduled for April 19-21. It would be a weekend affair, of course, and that was only if everything went according to plan.

"The show will be over, and you won't have to worry about leaving Carter anytime soon," Jen concluded.

"You're right!" I yelled in excitement.

Jen and I stayed up the rest of the night, eating cookies, brownies, and drinking wine until we eventually passed out.

CHAPTER 4
NIKA

It was the longest ride home ever after we pulled over. We were all quiet as I drove us back into the Seven Cities. Jen gave me a strange look when we were outside. I knew that look. She thought Sasha knew about our abortions. We told Lace because we shared everything, but considering how hard Sasha was trying to get pregnant, we did not share the information with her. Not that we did not want to; we just knew how it would make her feel.

Jen was quiet, and I was sure she was thinking about her next move with Robbie. My mind was so preoccupied thinking about how I might have fucked up my friendship with Lamar by sending him that text. I could not believe I had done that. "I need to apologize. I do not want Lamar thinking I am some type of home wrecker. I am the complete opposite. I hate cheaters. They are fucking cowards, cheaters, that is. They are too much of a coward to get out of a bad situation and find their true happiness. So, they stay in an unhappy situation, and they cheat.

I have become a coward. I know I am, but even knowing that, I will not dare put that on anyone else. What type of woman am I? Who does that? How would this change our friendship?" All these questions flooded my thoughts, and I did not have the answers to any of them. However, this ride gave me ample time to think about them all. I felt like I ruined the relationship between Lamar and me. Of course, I didn't know for sure, but I didn't want anything to come between our friendship.

I pulled up to Mom's house so Sasha and Jen could grab their kids. DD was spending the night. I needed time without her to wrap my head around everything. After everyone was safely buckled in, I headed home. I pulled up to the house and said my goodbyes to Sasha, Jen, and the little ones. Sasha got out of the back seat and into the driver's seat. She waved goodbye as I hesitated walking into the house. Jay had already sent me several texts, mostly about coming home to suck his scruffy dick.

Jay and I never talked. He made all the decisions and told me only what I needed to know. I think that was another reason I started growing closer to Lamar. We discussed everything, and he listened attentively when I spoke. Jay saw me through the window, taking my time to make it into the house, and yelled to get my attention. I looked up and saw him in the window motioning for me to come suck his dick. I hated Jay. I hated the way he treated me, I thought as I entered our apartment.

Jay had not even allowed me to settle before he had his pants down and legs open with his dick in his hand. "Come on over here, girl. I have been waiting on you all weekend," Jay demanded. "Asshole!" I thought. He always thought he was doing me a favor by letting me hang with my friends, and thus should be rewarded upon my return.

My interest in Lamar began to grow as my hatred for Jay grew. Particularly the day after he helped me with my tire, or maybe I was always interested and fought the feeling. I don't know if it was Lamar making sure I got home safely or Jay slapping the shit out of me that triggered my feelings for Lamar, but something that day sparked a liking.

I had fantasized about Lamar for so long that whenever I was instructed to suck Jay's dick, I considered it practice for the day I would finally have Lamar's dick in my mouth. I walked over to Jay and kneeled before him. I took his shaft into my mouth and imagined it was Lamar's. I thought about Lamar and how our relationship might change after that weekend. I imagined it changed for the better, adding a layer of intimacy reserved for just the two of us. I stroked Jay's dick up and down as I fantasized about Lamar. I did not even know if Lamar enjoyed oral sex, but I sucked Jay's dick as if Lamar truly enjoyed it. It gave me the feeling that even if Lamar did not like having his dick sucked, he would when I'd be done.

I was so immersed in my thoughts, I hadn't felt Jay's dick pulsate in my mouth, an indication that he was about to cum, and just at that moment, he came while I was in mid-stroke, sucking. Jay's sperm was disgusting. I was sure it was due to all the weed he smoked and the alcohol he drank. I imagined Lamar's sperm would be tasty, so I swallowed with the thought of Lamar in mind.

Jay was so turned on by me swallowing his nasty ass cum, he looked at me in disbelief as I looked up smiling. Little did he know I was not smiling at him. I knew I'd never fuck, suck, or make love to Lamar; therefore, I acted out all my desires and fantasies on Jay.

My pussy became wetter and began pulsating thinking of Lamar. Which was precisely what I needed if I was going to fuck Jay. Jay was a mean-ass bastard, and if I did not satisfy him, he made me pay for it for days to come. Jay remained seated on the sofa as I slid my pants off. I kept my shirt and bra on as there was really no need for me to get fully undressed. Sex with Jay was for Jay and Jay only.

I walked over to Jay and straddled him while he sat patiently waiting on the sofa. That was the only time Jay was patient. I rode Jay slowly with my eyes closed so I could picture Lamar. I put my arm around Jay's neck and lay my head on his bald head. I opened my eyes and kissed his bald head gently. Lamar also had a bald head. It was much easier for me to ride Jay, thinking about Lamar while looking only at Jay's bald head. I rode Jay until we both came. I climaxed in his lap with a smile on my face. I climbed off Jay, still thinking of Lamar, showered, and went to bed.

I woke up happy, imagining my husband was someone else. Then Jay ruined it by speaking. Of course, fussing about having to make a detour before work. When DD stayed over Mom's on a school night, we had to get up earlier to go over to Mom's and leave DD her daily letter.

It was something I got from my dad's wife. Whenever I stayed over on a school night, she would write me a letter and leave it for me to find in the morning. The letters were encouraging notes that reminded me to be my best and showed me that I was loved. I loved seeing those notes in the morning. My relationship with Mom was funny. But my relationship with my stepmom was strong and loving. My mom loved me when she was happy. My stepmother loved me always.

I started leaving DD the same type of letters before she could even read. I never wanted her to doubt my love for her. I wanted our relationship to be what I dreamed of having with my mother. I wanted DD to know true love from her mother. It was funny, though, because my mom's relationship with DD was the relationship I wanted with my mom. She was simply not capable of loving me that way at the time.

Although Mom stayed around the corner, it was always a hassle when I had to go there first. Jay liked to follow me into work, and he hated making the detour. It always caused an early morning argument. He could not understand why I needed to leave DD notes every morning, but it was something she had become used to, and I wanted to do. It was one of the things I absolutely would not budge on. Some mornings, not budging came at a cost.

I sometimes thought Jay was jealous of the relationship I had with DD, but that would be weird, right? I don't know; I just felt like he was off some days. He loved DD, of course, but his love for her was the same as for me, conditional. If Jay got what he wanted, then everything in life for our family fell perfectly into place. That even went for DD. I hated that she had to deal with Jay, but I could not leave him. I had made a commitment that I had to honor. That's why I allowed DD to stay at my mom's place so often. I tried to shield her as much as I could.

Jay followed me into work because he did not trust me, not because I had done anything wrong, but because he was constantly doing something wrong. So he always wanted to know my whereabouts. I stayed on my best behavior to avoid the wrath of Jay. My only male friend was Lamar, and Jay knew nothing about him. We had only recently become friends. We had always been cordial and friendly, but it recently evolved into an admirable friendship. I had also noticed that I had recently become very drawn to Lamar, something crazy. I did not understand quite what it was, but it was something.

I arrived at work after sitting in stupid traffic for over an hour. It was horrible coming onto the base now. We were still on high alert since the 911 attacks. I pulled into a parking spot at my squadron and sat in my car for a little while, thinking about seeing Lamar. I was nervous about seeing him since I sent him that inappropriate text while at Lace's house over the weekend. I was not sure if Lamar had decided to end our friendship over it. I truly enjoyed our friendship, and a part of me felt like I needed the daily escape from my real life.

I got myself together and finally got out of the car, heading inside. My time here was short. I was due to transfer the next month. I was staying in Norfolk, but was heading for a shore command, and thinking about that made me sad. I would no longer be able to see Lamar once I transferred. He was my daily peace. I walked inside and spoke to a few folks as I made my way to my cubicle. I contemplated going to the squadron's store, but opted not to. I wanted to hide away for a bit, but not for too long, so that I could get my nerves under control.

I sat at my desk and logged in. Once my computer was up and running, I opened my email. I was shocked to see that Lamar had already emailed me. I became super anxious. There was no subject, just three little periods. "WTF does that mean?" I wondered. I opened the email and felt a sigh of relief. "Lunch?" the email stated. I smiled and looked around to ensure no one could see my screen. I was so excited. I did not know why, but I was overwhelmed with excitement. It was crazy. Lamar and I had never gone to lunch before then. We usually just spent time talking in each other's cubicles. I could not respond fast enough. I felt my heart doing leaps in my chest as I typed, "Sure! What time?" and hit send. I sat there for a few moments in a complete daze.

I attempted to do some work while I waited for Lamar's response. I didn't have much to do since all my assignments had been assigned to other people. There were still two or more small assignments I was responsible for, but it was not enough to keep me busy. I started one of the assignments, and as soon as I was done, I heard footsteps creeping up behind me. I assumed it was my first class, so I swung around playfully in my chair and stared into Lamar's face. "Hey, are you ready?" he asked.

I turned back around to get a glimpse of the time. It was only a quarter to ten. "Do you want to go to lunch now?" I asked. "Yeah, unless you have work to do," Lamar responded. Seeing as I had absolutely nothing to do, I grabbed my wallet, and we headed for lunch.

"I'll drive," Lamar announced. I assumed we would drive separately. I was a little nervous to ride with Lamar, but I followed him anyway, not saying a word. As we walked toward his car, I could feel some anxiety building in my chest. Lamar must have smelled my fear. He looked over and smiled. "I got my car windows tinted over the weekend," he said as he opened the passenger car door for me to enter. As I sat inside, I heaved a heavy sigh of relief.

I had no idea where we were headed, and I did not ask. I loved spending time with him, and it did not matter where we ended up. Lamar drove off base and down Tidewater Drive and pulled up to a small sandwich shop, Sam's Texas Sub Shop.

"Have you ever been here?" I asked.

"No, have you?" Lamar responded.

"No, I haven't," I responded.

"Good, it'll be a first for both of us," Lamar said as he exited the car.

Sam's was a tiny sub shop. It appeared to be a neighborhood favorite. The counter was lined with bags of food waiting for pickup. "It must be good," I thought. I studied the menu closely, making sure to pick something good, as the workers continued to prepare for the lunch rush. Lamar did the same. Once my mind was made up, I walked to the counter to place my order. I reached into my wallet to pay. Lamar came over, touched my hand, and said, "I got it!" as he too placed his order. We chatted about nothing in particular while we waited for our food.

Once it was ready, Lamar motioned for us to leave. I was a little disappointed. I at least thought we would eat there. I had to remember I was the only one short on my time. I am sure Lamar had to get back to the office to do some work. "Do you want to eat in the Squadron's store?" I asked.

Lamar looked at me and smiled. "No, I was thinking we could go sit by the water and eat if you have time?"

My heart did backflips in my chest. I was trying so hard not to smile. I did not even look at Lamar when I answered "Sure, why not!"

Once we got back in the car, Lamar pulled out of the parking lot and took a left onto the highway on Tidewater Drive and headed west on 64. I had no idea where he was going since the water was east, so I sat and made small talk. I talked about my trip to Maryland, leaving out the parts about Lace being raped and us planning to kill a man. I also left out the part about me sending that text. Did not want to dive into that since the day was going so well. Lamar exited the highway and headed toward gate four. After entering the base, he swung his first right and followed the road until it ended at the water. Lamar parked on the side, and we exited the car, walking over to some questionable-looking benches.

"I never knew this was back here," I whispered. There were a few other sailors out, sitting on the grass, some on the benches, and some in the sand, eating, talking, or smoking. Everyone looked so relaxed.

"When we do our search and rescue training, I see this area from the water. One day after the training, I drove around until I found it. I know how much you like the water so I thought you would enjoy eating lunch here."

"You know me so well," I said with a smile.

Lamar and I sat, ate lunch, and talked for hours. I completely lost track of time, until he said it was time to go. It was past one pm by the time we were done. I didn't want our time together to end. I think Lamar could sense that, not that he would ever acknowledge it or comment on it, but I was sure he made a mental note. As we reached the car, Lamar opened my door for me to enter. Lamar stood there watching as I got comfortable in my seat. I looked up and saw him smiling, before I could speak, he said, "Thanks for the picture this weekend. I really enjoyed being able to see you outside of work in your own zone." I was dying on the inside and taking off guard by his comments. I didn't quite know what to say but words found their way out of my partially open mouth, "I thought I might have ruined our friendship by sending it," I whispered.

"I think we will be friends forever," Lamar said as he closed the passenger side door.

I couldn't help but smile. When Lamar got into the car, I thanked him for lunch, and we drove back to the command in silence. I was smiling like a schoolgirl. Lamar was straight-faced and serious as usual. "No problem," Lamar finally replied, "I enjoyed it. I hope we can do it again sometime." I literally wanted to jump out of my skin... the thought of spending more time with Lamar, sitting by the water, got me excited. Being near him always made my pussy super wet but spending uninterrupted time with him today made my pussy throb.

It wasn't about sex though. Well, not just sex, of course, I desired to have sex with him, but I knew that was out of the question. Nonetheless, I was falling for Lamar, I thought. I couldn't be too sure, but I knew I had the strongest desires to be with him, in his presence, near him as close as possible all the time and when I wasn't with him, I thought of him nonstop.

CHAPTER 5
JEN

Considering Robbie's actions, the other Thursday, I was surprised at how well I'd been sleeping. It's like I hadn't even thought about Robbie or my section leader. Well, I had that one though while I was washing Lace up but for the most part, my mind was clear. Well, not clear, but not on Robbie's stupid ass. I knew I couldn't afford to move out, and I couldn't afford for Robbie to leave, since I'd soon be jobless.

My time was short in the Navy, and my supervisor was cool as a fan. He allowed me to take extra nursing classes during the day so I could finish my nursing program early. Normally, I would go to work around 7 am then head for my first class at 11 am, but since I was still at Sasha's house and simply just didn't feel like it, I decided not to go to work that day. I called my supervisor and told him I had some medical stuff to do. He didn't care, his time was short, too. My supervisor and I were both scheduled to separate from the Navy within days of each other. He pretty much let me do whatever I wanted at this point, as he did the same.

I thought a little more about my next moves while I made a pot of coffee to have with my brownie. I could hear the kids upstairs talking and playing and the thought of their innocence made me smile.

"What are you smiling at?" Sasha asked as she entered the kitchen. "The sound of the kids playing—their joy brought me a slight piece of happiness," I responded.

"I'm staying with Robbie," I continued.

Sasha sat silently and waited for me to add something more to the comment. I blabbered for a little, explaining my position before Sasha interrupted me. "Jen, I understand! It's hard starting over, especially when kids are involved. You know I love you and will support any decision you make. I just want you to make the right decision for you. That's all!" Sasha concluded.

I knew Sasha would understand, support, and respect my decision. Nika would, too. The only person who would have something to say was Lace, but luckily, I wouldn't have to explain myself to Lace as I hadn't even mentioned the Robbie incident to her.

I headed home shortly after Sasha and I had a cup of coffee and a few too many brownies. Alisha was happy to be heading home. She missed her dad. If only she knew what an asshole he was.... We arrived in record time. Robbie wasn't there, of course, but Alisha wanted to talk to him. I called Robbie at work so Alisha could speak with him. I didn't know what the hell they were talking about. I zoned out looking at my house. It was exactly the way I left it. That frying pan I threw was still lying where it landed, and food was splattered against the wall. That son of a bitch didn't even clean up. "What an asshole!" I thought.

Alisha finished her call and handed me the phone. I hung it up and had started to clean when I heard the phone ring. I answered it, and it was Robbie's dumb ass. "Jen, we need to talk! Don't you think?" Robbie asked. "There's nothing to talk about, Robbie. I'll see you when you get home," I responded as I hung the phone up again. I wasn't going to waste my time talking to Robbie or even explaining my decision to stay to him. He wasn't even worth the conversation.

I went through the house, picked up the pan, and scrubbed the food off the wall. After that, I started in the bedroom. This fool still had the same sheets on the bed. I removed them and put them in the washer and started the machine. Then it dawned on me that I would never use those sheets again. I stopped the washer, grabbed the sheets out, walked outside, and put them in the dumpster. I went back inside and continued cleaning. I was just finishing up my cleaning when I heard the patio door open. It was Robbie. This fucking idiot walked in with a dozen of fresh-cut roses. "Did this fool really think flowers would fix anything?"

Robbie was full of apologies, pushing those stupid ass roses in my face. I grabbed the roses and put them down the garbage disposal one by one while he stood there looking fucking foolish. I didn't say one word to Robbie. There was fucking NOTHING to say.

Robbie continued to beg over the next few hours as I continued my daily routine. I sat at the table and logged into my hybrid class discussion board. I did a few posts and a homework assignment. When I was done, I made dinner. Alisha and I sat at the table and ate. We then watched a little TV, and I gave Alisha her bath and put her down for bed. Robbie's ass was still begging. I finally looked at Robbie and said: "I'm not leaving. If you would like to leave, feel free, but I'm staying here. You are free to do as you wish with whom you wish!"

Clearly, that wasn't what Robbie wanted to hear. He couldn't believe I was so cold, and he turned on the faucet of alligator tears. I was revolted by Robbie. He literally made me sick, so sick that my stomach became queasy, and my mouth began to water, and before I knew it, I had puked all over Robbie.

It was then that he finally stopped begging and got the fuck out of my face.

MRS.THOMPSON

I wasn't happy with the plan the girls came up with. I thought it was too risky. There were so many different scenarios of how this could turn out badly. I tried pointing them out while the girls were still here, but they knew it all and didn't want to hear anything from me. Although they were all over 21, I felt like I was the only adult in the room. I needed to convince Lace to do the right thing. I supported her decision originally not to go to the cops, but after sleeping on it, I felt like it's the right thing to do. Antoinette's case wasn't handled correctly, but she lived on base. Lace was off base, surely local law enforcement would handle things differently. It's conflicting. I'd been through it before, and I didn't want Lace to experience the same thing, but I also didn't want her to get herself locked up.

"I'll catch Lace before heading to work," I thought, as I headed next door. Lace wasn't dressed for work; instead, she was sitting on the sofa while T ate breakfast at the coffee table.

"Good morning!" Lace exclaimed as I walked through the door.
"Good morning, Lace! Are you not working today?" I asked.

Lace didn't say a word; she simply shook her head no. Lace's face was still very swollen. Her eyes were open, but you could tell that there had been some type of trauma. After a few silent moments, Lace spoke, "I called in. I told my First-Class T had a fever and couldn't go to day care. That should give me two more days and time enough for some of the swellings to subside, or at least I hope so," Lace concluded with questing eyes. Noticing Lace wanted some reassurance, I offered it to her, "I'm sure two days of rest will help, Lace!"

I decided to stay with Lace for the day. I felt like she needed me there. She hadn't told anyone what happened besides me and the girls. I wanted Lace to call her mom, but Lace didn't want to, and after hearing what I had gone through, she was certainly not interested in putting her mother through that suffering. A part of me wished I hadn't shared my story with Lace, but the other part of me knew I had to.

Antoinette had told me once that harassment and rape were common in the military and often swept under the rug, but I didn't want to believe it. But now I knew it must be true. Jen described some painful moments she had to endure from asshole men in the Navy. My heart broke as each of them shared a story of their own, and to think it was the era of zero-tolerance.

48

I figured I would take the day and try and convince Lace to go to the cops. "I've been thinking, Lace. I think we should go to the cops. Incidents like this can take a mental toll on one, and I think that's the biggest factor you guys are leaving out of your plan. I just don't think you are mentally strong enough to carry this out. Let's not forget about the guilt you and your friends will endure for killing someone. Taking a human life. It will tear you apart. Plus, the handling of your case will more than likely be significantly different, since you were not on base when it happened. Let's try to do the right thing first, and then if that doesn't work, let's move forward with your plan?" I begged.

Lace had decided the previous night that she would no longer cry or show any signs of weakness when it came to this incident. She listened to me intently, but I could tell she was not hearing me. I laid out all the holes in their plan and continued to beg her to do the right thing and consider that she still had a child to raise.

Lace completely and utterly disagreed. She was adamant about dishing out her own justice. She had a plan and she was ready to put it in motion.

"My mind is made," Lace announced. Lace got up from the sofa, walked toward me as confident as only Lace could, and hugged me tightly. "Momma," Lace sometimes called me momma when she thought I was acting too much like her mother, "everything will be fine. I promise you; plus, I can't back down now. This is bigger than me and Antoinette. This is for every young girl who joins the military trying to change their life but is met by a male chauvinistic, dominating, sexist asshole!" Lace concluded.

At that moment, I knew there was nothing else I could do or say to change Lace's mind.

LACE

It's been 6 days since the attack, and I was finally starting to look like myself again. Mrs. Thompson has been a lifesaver, helping with T. She stayed home with me both days. The rest really did help, but I was ready to get out of this house. Every time I went into my bedroom, I thought about that asshole. As strong as I wanted to be, I couldn't. "Carlos took something from me. Something I'll never get back. I can't stand feeling powerless and sitting in this house intensifies that feeling."

Today would be my first day back to work and presumably my first day seeing Carlos again. The plan was to act as if nothing happened. Get Carlos to believe I didn't remember it was he that raped me. Confide in him about the rape and make him believe I was too drunk to remember what had happened. Even cry on his shoulder if I had to get him to believe me. Then in a few weeks, I would lure him back to my house and we would fucking torture him over the course of the weekend until he was too weak to fight back and then bury him alive in the woods behind his own house.

Mrs. Thompson was taking T to day care, so I only needed to focus on me today. I showered while all these crazy thoughts went through my head. The attack kept replaying in my mind, causing the pain and fear to resurface much too often. I know I was supposed to be strong and not cry but I just couldn't help it. I didn't cry in front of anyone, though. I cried silently and only when I was alone. I had become a complete wreck. "I'll wear makeup," I thought. That should help hide the bruises that aren't completely healed that people can see. There were so many other bruises all over my body. I became consumed in anger, thinking about the bruises he left me with, thinking about the plan he plotted against me. He had me move my gun because he had this planned, and he knew he was going to rape me, maybe that's why he paid for dinner first. The thought of that made me sick.

After my shower, I dressed quickly in the uniform of the day. I carefully applied my makeup, ensuring bruised areas were all covered. I pulled my hair back into a tight bun and placed my stud earrings in my ear. I gave myself a full once-over and was pleased with how I pulled myself together. It was game time, and I was ready.

I arrived at work, a little past 8 am, and purposely late for muster. I walked to my desk, got settled and logged in, and checked my email. Normally, Carlos emailed me every morning. We talked every day but since the rape, he hadn't called me and I him. I didn't see any emails from him for the past two days and none this morning. Knowing I had to convince him all was well, I drafted an email that simply read: "Good morning... out of sight out of mind huh? T was sick, so I was out Friday, Monday, and Tuesday. Let's have lunch if you're up for it."

I finished checking my email which took over an hour and still there was no reply. I started to think, "What if he's not dumb enough to fall for it?" I had to force myself not to think like that. I needed him to fall for it badly. I needed revenge. I started working on some tasks that had been assigned to me while I was out. I was in deep thought thinking about the automatic link system when I felt someone touch my shoulder. I turned around in my chair and it was Carlos. Fear crippled me, but I hoped he hadn't seen it. I smiled. Stood up and hugged him. He was shocked. He looked like he had seen a ghost. "What's up? Why didn't you email me back?" I asked in a light and friendly tone. Carlos didn't reply; instead, he just looked at me. I saw him looking at the bruises he left. I gave Carlos a weary smile and whispered, "Random gone wrong, really wrong. It was horrible, but I don't want to talk about it."

"Did you call the cops?" Carlos asked. Now, why the fuck was that the first thing he asked? He should have asked if I was OK, but the motherfucker was only concerned with himself!

"No, I didn't. I honestly don't remember what happened. I just remember walking him out. The next thing I knew, I was waking up in my hallway on the first floor, beaten and bruised. We were drinking. I don't know what happened. I don't remember enough to tell the cops, nor do I know the guy for real. All I have is a phone number, and I'm sure he has tossed that phone by now," I concluded.

"Lace, I've told you about those random ass men in and out of your house," Carlos said as he came in for a hug. I hugged him tightly and long, reassuring him that I didn't suspect him of anything.

Carlos released me as I whispered, "I'm scared. I never thought anything like this would happen to me," I said through quivering lips. The anger on the inside of me was boiling. There was NO WAY in hell I would be able to keep this up for two weeks. I cried full-blown tears right there in front of Carlos. My tears weren't fake, though. I cried, thinking about him raping me and thinking he could get away with it. I cried so hard, I got the attention of my supervisor, certainly not on purpose.

My supervisor took note, walked over, and asked, "What's wrong, Petty Officer Miles?" Before I could answer, Carlos whispered something in his ear, presumably, what I had just shared with him. My supervisor looked at me, shook his head, and said, "I'm sure it was well deserved. You walk around here being all giddy and flirtatious, thinking you can just tease men, and nothing happens. Hope you learned your lesson," he continued. "Take her home, Sargent!" my supervisor demanded while looking at me. "We don't need you here looking like that. And go to medical and get tested!" he yelled as he walked away.

I was absolutely paralyzed with rage. My mind started going crazy. The thoughts were out of control. The fucking insolence! "I'm going to make that motherfucker pay, too," I thought silently.

"I drove in," I whimpered through trembling lips. I was infuriated. Everything in me was on fire. "I'll follow you home, Lace," Carlos announced. I didn't want that motherfucker anywhere near my house until I was ready to kill him. But I couldn't respond like that if our plan was going to be successful. My mind wanted to stay on track, but my body wanted to kill him there and then.

I gathered my things and Carlos went across the hall and gathered his things. We walked out to his car, and he drove me to my car. The anger was boiling over at this point. Carlos pulled up next to my car. As I opened the car door to exit, Carlos rested his hand on my thigh and assured me: "I'll be right behind you, Lace!"

I smiled sheepishly at Carlos, through tears of anger, and got out of his car and into mine. I tried to pray once I was seated, and I asked God for patience and strength as I attempted to carry out this plan. But I couldn't get my prayer out. I was too upset. I drove home slowly trying to calm myself. I wasn't expecting to be alone with Carlos so soon. I thought it would have taken at least a few days. "It was the fucking crying," I thought. But I couldn't hold it in, I was so angry. And weak. "I am too weak," I thought. Now this bastard would be in my fucking house, and I didn't even have a gun to protect myself from him. I screamed as loud as I could as I drove home.

I pulled up to my parking spot, and Carlos pulled in right beside me. I put my car in park and again tried hard to pray.

"Dear heavenly Father, give me the...." my prayer was quickly interrupted with "Fuck that nigga! He's fucking dying today. I don't give a fuck! Fuck the plan and fuck Carlos too!" I got out of the car and walked to the door. Carlos met me there. Asshole waited for me to use my key, and I wondered why he didn't just let himself in?

I opened the door, and we entered the house. We removed our boots as we always did when we entered. "I wonder if he took his shoes off the night he raped me," I thought. The house was now completely clean, thanks to my friends. Nothing like how Carlos left it early Friday morning. Carlos took note of the house being cleaned as if nothing had ever happened there. I went to the sofa and sat in the corner, my favorite spot. Carlos sat next to me, uncomfortably too close. My insides stewed; I could feel the change in my temperature as I sat there. "I'm scared," I whispered. "I could have sworn I let my random out and locked the door behind me. I don't know how he could have gotten back in. Although, I don't remember completely because I was drinking. I should have never had drinks with him," I cried.

"Did you leave him alone at any point? Maybe he unlocked the sliding door or the basement door when you excused yourself." I looked at Carlos in disbelief. Not because I thought what he was saying might be true, but the fact that this motherfucking nigga had the valor to play on my fucking intelligence. That shit incensed me.

"I'm going to go check the basement and make sure everything is closed and locked," Carlos said as he stood up and walked toward the basement.

Carlos opened the basement door and started walking and something inside of me clicked at that moment. And I lunged at him using all my strength and some strength I didn't know I had and pushed him down the steps. I stood there in shock for a moment as I watched him tumble down the thirteen steps screaming. He wasn't dead, but he was hurt.

I grabbed the first thing I saw, the iron poker lying next to my fireplace. I ran down the stairs as fast as I could before Carlos was able to get up. I swung the poker at Carlos and hit his head and back repeatedly. I cried and screamed with every strike until the poker bent. I contemplated running upstairs for a knife or something but was scared Carlos wasn't incapacitated enough. I ran into the laundry room and found a 2x4 left behind by one of the contracts. I grabbed it and raced back out to the stairway landing and continued striking Carlos until he finally stopped moving. He wasn't dead, though. He was still breathing. It was faint but breathing, nonetheless.

I was exhausted and my uniform was soaked in blood. I stood against the wall and slid down and landed in a pool of blood, Carlos' blood. I was still so very angry thinking about Carlos raping me. I turned Carlos over and unbuckled his pants and yanked his pants and boxers down. I then turned Carlos back onto his stomach, and I grabbed the broken and bent poker and shoved it up his ass with force and vigor. Carlos clinched and began to moan or cry. I'm not sure which one it was. I didn't care. I repeated the action, shoving the poker repeatedly until my arm began to hurt. I could still hear Carlos doing something, what, I wasn't sure. Carlos was bleeding profusely from his ass.

There was blood everywhere. I looked around the basement and screamed. But I couldn't stop myself. I picked the 2x4 up again and beat him over and over again until I no longer had strength in my arms.

When I was finished, I looked around and realized I had fucked up badly. This was surely not part of the plan. "There is no way I will be able to hide this," I thought as I began to cry and panic. I slid down the wall again landing not too far from Carlos. He wasn't moving, still breathing, though. I don't know how long I sat there before I heard the front door being unlocked.

"Lace, you here?" Mrs. Thomson yelled. I didn't respond at first. I didn't want her to know what I had done. I sat motionlessly and quietly, although I was in the basement and there was no way she could see me. I heard her yell out again, "Lace, where are you? I see your car, and I see Carlos' car. Answer me, Lace?"

I thought about not responding, but then I thought about the fact that she saw Carlos' car and thought she might really be worried. Then I heard the T's little voice yell, "Mommy! Mom, where are you?" It was then I decided to answer.

"Mom!" I yelled with a squeaky voice. "I'm down here. Please don't bring T down."

I heard the panic in her footsteps as she rushed toward the basement following my voice. I hadn't moved. I was literally still sitting in the exact spot where I slid down the side of the wall and landed after beating Carlos with the 2x4. I felt her presence before I heard her. Mrs. Thompson screamed my name as loud as she could, and I jumped. "Lace, what have you done?" she asked.

CHAPTER 6
MRS.THOMPSON

I couldn't believe what I was looking at. I was dumbfounded and paralyzed as I stood at the top of the stairway. The basement looked like a massacre scene from where I stood. I heard little footsteps, and I turned and rushed toward T. I grabbed him and hurried out of the house yelling, "I'll be back, Lace! I'm taking him next door." I ran across the grass to my house. I was panicky and sweating. Hubby didn't have a clue about anything that had gone on at Lace's house. I didn't tell him. He thought of Lace as a daughter, too, and I was scared of how he might have reacted if he found out Lace, too, had been raped. So, I didn't say a word. But with this mess Lace made, I didn't know if I should say something to him now. There's no way Lace and I would be able to cover this up without some help.

I rushed into the house feeling anxious. I immediately calmed myself so hubby wouldn't think anything. I held T in my arms as I walked over to hubby who was sitting in his rocker. I planted a wet kiss on his forehead. "I brought you a playmate," I said jokingly. More so for myself than him. I was nervous, and I felt like hubby could see through me. "I'm going to go help Lace with something. I'll be back shortly," I said as I rushed back out of the house.

As I entered Lace's house, fright set right back in. I didn't know what we were going to do. I walked back over to the top of the basement stairs and saw lace standing over Carlos. She was completely naked. Lace had found rope from one of the contractor's bins that had been left in the basement and tied up Carlos' hands and legs.

"Is he dead?" I asked as I crept down the stairs.

"He's still breathing," Lace responded without looking up.

"Did he kill Antoinette?" I queried

"I'm sorry, I didn't get a chance to ask. It all happened so fast. It wasn't my intent. I just got so angry and impulse took over," Lace continued as she walked toward me. "I'm going to shower!"

"Wait, Lace! Stay there. Let me bring you a towel so you don't track the blood," I demanded. I grabbed several towels out of the linen closet. Lace layered the stairs and used the final towel to clean her feet. "Lace, you can't just leave him there. What are you going to do? What's your plan?"

Lace didn't answer me; instead, she walked her naked ass up the flight of stairs, into the bathroom, and into the shower. I stared at the basement, contemplating walking down to see how bad it was. From the top, it looked horrible. I didn't know what she was thinking about. "How does she plan to fix this?" I pondered.

Carlos was just lying there hog-tied, barely breathing. I got halfway down the stairs and got sick to my stomach. I hurried back up the few steps I had come down. I walked over and sat on the sofa, thinking or trying to think, I didn't know what to do. Then I remembered Carlos' car was still outside. We needed to get rid of his car. "I'll follow Lace in my car, and we'll take Carlos' car and park it at his house," I thought. I looked around to see if by chance Carlos' keys were upstairs. I was hoping and praying they were. I didn't want either of us to have to go back downstairs until we figured out a plan. I sat there thinking long and hard before I picked up the phone and called Sasha.

Sasha answered on the second ring, I could tell she was busy, so I spoke fast and clear. "Sasha darling, remember the show you guys were coming up to see?" I didn't even wait on a response, I just continued. "It's been fast-tracked due to an impulsive response, and it's a mess. Worse than anything I have ever seen or could have imagined. You guys might miss it if you don't get up here soon," I concluded.

Sasha was at a loss for words. She tried to speak but kept getting tongue-tied. When she was finally able to put words together, she informed me that there was no way she would make the show that night or the following day. "It's Wednesday, I can't leave here until Friday. I have to work and take care of Mason. What was she thinking?" Sasha continued. "I'll call Jen and Nika and see if they can make it. If so, I'll watch the kids here and then come up Friday evening."

I hung up from Sasha and went to check on Lace. She had finished showering and was lying across the bed, naked and fast asleep.

"Lace, get the hell up!" I yelled. Lace jumped up dazed. "We have got to get this guy's car out of here. Why are you sleeping?"

"I'm exhausted," Lace responded as she lay back down without a care in the world.

"Lace, get up! We need to get his car back to his place. I'll follow you in my car and park around the back. Just as you guys planned. You'll wear all black, park his car, go into his house, and drop off his keys, wallet, and phone. Leave out the back door and meet me in the alley. Do you remember that part of the plan, Lace?" I asked, struggling to keep her attention.

Lace got up and did as she was instructed. While she was dressing, we had to tweak the original plan. The girls were supposed to be Lace's alibi just in case she was questioned, but since they weren't here, I would need to be Lace's alibi. We decided I would take my phone home to give the impression that I was home all evening and could vouch that Lace was home as well. Lace would call Sasha before we left, and they would leave both phones on until we returned.

Carlos was much bigger than Lace, so she had to wear layers to look the part. He was also a tad bit taller, but we figured in the dark if anyone saw her, it would be from afar, and they wouldn't be able to tell the difference. Lace outfitted in several hoodies, with a black hoodie on top and three pairs of sweatpants. She wore five or six pairs of socks to keep her feet from sliding as she would wear Carlos' boots back to his house. Once Lace was fully draped, I gave her a once-over to make sure everything was in place.

"I'm ready!" Lace announced. Then it hit me, "We don't have his keys, wallet, or cell phone," I said.

"Shit!" Lace yelled. Lace removed all her clothes until she was completely naked again. We walked downstairs together and then to the basement door. We peeked in to make sure Carlos was still there, and he was, still barely breathing. Lace walked down the steps until she was directly over Carlos. She searched all his pockets until she found everything we needed.

The items were soaked in blood. I grabbed a towel for Lace's feet. She cleaned her feet while I grabbed a dishtowel from the kitchen. I took the items from Lace before she stepped out of the basement, to prevent the blood from dripping. Lace went back upstairs, washed up quickly, and put back on her layers of clothing. I dropped the keys in a bucket with bleach and water, until all the blood was removed. The phone and wallet I wiped down as best I could. Once I was done, I put all the items in a zip lock bag to make sure we didn't leave any fingerprints on them.

Lace and I were finally ready to head out. She called Sasha as we planned and left her phone on the dining room table. We got in the respective cars and headed for Carlos' house. He lived in Seven Oaks, which was only about a fifteen-minute drive.

Seven Oaks was a new and upcoming neighborhood. Only a few of the houses had been built and the rest of the wooded area had yet to be developed. Lace turned down the street of Carlos' house, and I turned the street behind it and waited for Lace. As I sat there, I couldn't help but wonder what I had gotten myself into.

Lace should have come out immediately, but I found myself sitting there for far too long. I began to get nervous. I sat there for another fifteen minutes. Fifteen minutes turned to 30 minutes quickly and still no Lace.

JEN

Alisha and I were developing new routines, without Robbie. Not that he had left or anything. He was still in the apartment; I just no longer did anything for or with Robbie. It was almost as if someone flipped a switch in my brain. It was so easy for me to distance and separate myself from anything remotely related to him. I spent time with Alisha without Robbie and if he wanted to spend time with her, he would have to do it without me. Normally, we would all eat dinner together, and after dinner, we'd have family quality time, whatever that consisted of for the day. Sometimes it would be playing a game together, watching a movie, and or reading a book. But now, I no longer entertained any of that foolishness.

This is Alisha's and my third day going for an after-dinner walk. It was nice. We both got the chance to work off the food we ate. I had seen parents who worked out with their young kids and always thought it was weird. I figured you couldn't really focus on getting the exercise you need if your kid was in tow, but honestly, it was fine. Alisha ran ahead most of the time and when she was tired, which was often, she climbed back in her stroller, lay back and relaxed, while I walked or jogged.

Just as I bent the corner to make it into the house, my cell phone rang. It was Sasha. I debated answering it and decided not to. I was in my zen and didn't feel like being bothered. Not that we were beefing or anything, I just wanted to remain in my peaceful realm at the moment. Sasha called again and again. After the third time, I realized I was not going to be left alone to be one with my zen this evening.

"Hey, girlie! What's good?" I said as I answered the phone.

Sasha and Nika were both on the line, hysterically rambling on and on. Occasionally, I was able to pick up a few words here and there and learned that we were on the verge of missing the show.

"Jay is on duty tonight. I can swing by and pick you up and then we can head up to Lace's tonight. Can you leave tonight, Jen?" Nika shouted over Sasha.

Unsure of what exactly was going on, I asked Nika to come over so we could discuss in person.

Nikka arrived while I was bathing Alisha. She walked in straight past Robbie without speaking. "That's right. If I don't speak to him, we don't speak to him. Fuck him! That's the way it is." Nika walked into the bathroom and closed the door behind her so we could talk in private.

"All I know is Lace jumped the gun and needs help cleaning up the mess. That's really all Sasha could get out. I brought Jay's gun, too!" Nika concluded.

"Why did you bring Jay's gun?" I asked.

"I don't think Carlos is actually dead, from what I gathered from Sasha," Nika responded.

I was so confused and was tempted to ask more questions, but I opted not to. Robbie was still in the other room, and I didn't want him to know anything. I finished with Alisha, got her out of the tub, and ready for bed. I read her a bedtime story, although I wasn't sure if I was reading or shouting. I attempted to rock Alisha to sleep. I knew it was a horrible habit to start, but I enjoyed it just as much as she did. But I couldn't do it that night, my nerves were getting the best of me. I was anxious and trembling. I handed Alisha off to Robbie. I spoke with Robbie quickly and told him my plans for the weekend. I also reminded him of his parental responsibilities. Robbie had forgotten Alisha more than a handful of times at day care, so I often had to remind him when I had evening class or duty to pick her up from day care. Sasha had agreed to pick Alisha up Friday and drop her with Mrs. Rodgers if I hadn't made it back by the time she headed up for MD. I then packed a small bag of clothes and two pairs of coveralls.

Nika and I hit the road soon as I was done packing. Shortly after Nika hit the highway, I started to relax, not a lot but just enough to roll a joint. Once my joint was rolled, I lit it up and took a few puffs. Smoking relaxed me. I was the only one that smoked and had just picked up the habit recently. Once I started talking or maybe rambling, it was as if the floodgates opened. I talked almost the entire ride about Robbie and me. I was still very hurt by Robbie's actions although I hadn't talked about them much. There was some uncertainty before I walked in on Robbie about the state of our relationship—I wasn't completely naïve. I wasn't completely blind, though I wasn't a hundred percent sure of what it could be. But I knew something was off between us. I just thought we were growing apart. I never imagined he would fuck someone in our bed.

Nika hadn't heard the details of that night. The car ride was the first time I went into details about the Robbie situation. Nika became livid, hearing about me walking in on Robbie and that bitch. It was as if my heartbreak fueled her.

MRS. THOMSPON

I began to worry and just as I was about to get out of the car, Lace came walking toward the car. She was shocked. Her face looked as if she had seen a ghost. "What's wrong? Did anyone see you? What took you so long? Lace, answer me!" I said all at one time without waiting on responses to any of my questions.

"Just drive!" Lace asked sternly. Considering the situation, I didn't scold Lace; instead, I started to drive. As we drove in silence, Lace lifted her top sweatshirt and pulled out a medium-sized black leather box.

"That's what took you so long? You were stealing from him? You stole his watches?" I yelled. Still asking question after question without waiting on an answer. Lace looked at me with eyes full of tears.

"It's not a watch box. I didn't even know what I was looking for when I started searching his closets. Something in my gut just told me to do it. And I searched everything and everywhere as quickly as I could. This was hidden in the back of his closet next to my gun. I think it's a trophy box. Items collected from his other victims," Lace concluded.

My heart literally dropped in my chest. "How many other victims? Is anything in there from Antoinette?" I asked through quivering lips.

"I don't know," Lace responded. "We'll have to go through it when we get home."

It was the longest fifteen-minute ride ever. I couldn't stop thinking about what I might find in that box. "What if there were other boxes? What if Lace overlooked something in her rush?" I thought to myself. "We should go back," I announced. "We can't. I left the keys and locked the door just as we planned." "Of all the times to follow the plan you chose this time? Were there any other boxes, Lace? What if you missed something?"

"If I missed something, then I'm sure the cops will find it," Lace responded clearly tired of my questions. We arrived back at the house and I couldn't get inside quickly enough to go through the box.

We walked inside the house, and it was almost frightening. You could hear Carlos from the basement. His moans had become louder and more intense. Lace's face became bloodshot with every moan. She dropped the box on the floor as she rushed to get her gun out of the case. Once she finally got the case open, Lace ran downstairs. I wasn't sure what she was going to do because I was too invested in going through the box that had fallen. I couldn't ask, nor could I stop her.

I started gathering the fallen items when I heard Lace scream. I ran to the basement door as she was coming back up the stairs. "He took the bullets out. There're no fucking bullets!" Lace began to scream and yell until her screams turned into sobs. Lace dropped the gun where she stood and fell into my arms. "What are we going to do?" Lace asked through tears. "We'll figure it out!" I assured her. "Go get changed, Lac!"

Lace headed upstairs while I finished gathering the items that had fallen from the box. I heard the shower turn on as I stared at the items. None of the items looked familiar to me. My heart started beating faster and faster as I searched and searched for anything of Antoinette's in the box and nothing in the box was hers. Nothing looked even remotely familiar to me. I heard the shower turn off and Lace fumbling around upstairs. Within minutes, she was back downstairs. Lace picked up her gun case where it had fallen when she opened it.

Lace walked over to me where I sat in her favorite spot on the couch and handed me a handful of items. This was stuffed in my case. As the items fell into my hand, I felt my heart stop. Among other things, Lace dropped a solid gold ring with a princess cut emerald stone. I felt the inside of the ring to see if it was engraved, and it was. My heart started to beat slowly but purposeful. I knew the ring belonged to Antoinette. It was the one we bought her for her 16th birthday. She always wore it. When she was found, the ring was missing. After running my fingers across the engraved words multiple times, I turned the ring around to read the message engraved inside it: "You'll always be our princess," it read. I repeated those words over and over until I could no longer form words.

I sat there silently. I could see Lace watching me, but she didn't say a thing. "I'm going to stay until Jen and Nika arrive, and then I'm going to head home. I will keep T with me for the night, while you figure out what you're going to do," I said, breaking my silence.

I don't know how long we must have sat there in silence. At some point, Lace finally walked over to me. "Is that Antoinette's?" Lace asked. I didn't answer. I wanted to but I couldn't. "It's beautiful," Lace continued. With everything Lace was going through, she was still able to have compassion and empathy for me. She placed her hand on my hand and laid her head on my shoulder. "Everything is going to be alright, Mama. I'm going to take care of it. He will never hurt anyone again!"

Lace was eerily calm. I didn't know what was scarier, hearing how calm she was or knowing that there was a rapist and killer downstairs fighting for his life?

CHAPTER 7
NIKA

We arrived at Lace's house later than expected. At some point, I must have been driving slower than I thought. I'm sure it was during the time I was absorbing Jen's story. Sitting there, listening to Jen, made me want to put Robbie on the list next. "I can't believe how these men treat us. What have we done to be treated so badly?" I questioned.

We pulled up to Laces' and parked in visitor parking. We both exited the car at the same time. I grabbed my bag, and Jen did the same. Walking up to Lace's house made me nervous. I wasn't sure what we were about to walk into. Jen grabbed my hand as we walked up, side by side, both frightened beyond belief. The door swung open as we got closer, but no one was at the door. I peeked in and saw Lace walking back toward the sofa where Mrs. Thompson was in Lace's favorite spot. Jen and I entered slowly. I closed and locked the door behind me. Jen dropped her bag on the stairway landing. I held onto my bag.

The house was dark, while Mrs. Thompson sat silently, holding something tightly in her hand. Lace sat next to her, comforting her.

"What happened?" I asked.

"I just snapped," Lace responded.

"Is he dead?" Jen questioned

Lace didn't respond; instead, she shook her head no and sat back on the sofa.

"Well, what's the plan, Lace? What do you want to do?" Jen asked.

"We took Carlos' car back to his house. I found my gun and a box with women's items in it. I took the box," Lace continued.

As Lace was speaking, I could hear moans.

"Is that him?" Jen asked.

"Yes," Lace responded as she continued.

In the box was this ring. Lace grabbed Mrs. Thompson's hand and opened it for us to see. It was a beautiful gold ring.

"Did it belong to Antoinette?" Jen asked.

As everyone was talking about the ring, Carlos' moans became louder. I'm not sure if it was in real life or in my head, but his moans were hunting me as I stood there. It was as if every time he moaned, I lost my breath. I began to get hot, dizzy, and sweaty. I felt like I was going to pass out. The moans became overwhelming. They were literally the only thing I could hear. And at some point, I must have blacked out.

"What the fuck!" Jen yelled as I felt her shaking me. I investigated Jen's face which was full of fright, then I looked down at Carlos whom I now happened to be standing over. I held Jay's smoking gun in my hand, and there was a bullet hole in the back of Carlos' head. I screamed as Jen was searching my face for answers. I didn't even remember coming downstairs, so there was no way I could provide answers to the questions she was searching for. I was just as confused as Jen. Anxiety began to build in my stomach. I became hysterical, crying in a panic.

I wanted to stay in the moment of denial, but realizing what I had done, something came over me, and I kicked into action mode.

"Fuck it! What's done is done. It's time to clean up the mess now!" I said to Jen while she was still dazed and confused.

Jen was still in shock. Lace and Ms. Thompson never made it downstairs. I grabbed Jen, and we ran upstairs. Lace stopped us at the top of the stairs. "Wait here!" she insisted.

While Lace was grabbing garbage bags from the kitchen, I yelled: "I shot him! He's dead! There's blood everywhere. We need to get him out of here!" I demanded.

Lace lined the floor with garbage bags. "Walk on the bags only!" she instructed.

Mrs. Thompson stared at me, not sure exactly what to say or do. No one knew the next move. We hadn't planned anything out. But we needed to make a move and get Carlos' dead body the fuck out of here. While everyone stared in silence, I went into the kitchen and grabbed a handful of garbage bags from Lace's pantry, and headed downstairs. Jen followed closely behind me. I took one bag and lifted one leg at a time and placed it in the bag. Once the legs were secure, I moved onto his upper body.

Carlos wasn't a huge guy, but he was much bigger than us. I couldn't figure out how to fully cover his body. It took me a minute and then Jen suggested we cut a hole in the bag and pull it down to cover the middle portion of his body. So that's what we did: I cut the bag and slid it over top of him. There was so much blood, though. Shit was slippery and sticky as hell. It was everywhere. Together, Jen and I managed to lift him and put him inside. It's amazing what one could do when the adrenaline was rushing through one's bones.

Now we had to figure out where we would dump his body and how we would transfer it. Although he was wrapped in the garbage bags, the bags were now covered in blood.

Jen and I stood there contemplating for quite some time. We were silent in our thoughts when I noticed lights shining in the back of Lace's house. I started to panic as the lights got closer and closer to the house.

"Who the fuck could that be?" I asked.

"I don't know!" Jen responded, looking just as frightened as me.

As we stood there frozen in fear, we saw a shadow walking toward the basement door. I couldn't make out who it was, and I couldn't figure out why anyone would be coming to Lace's basement. The shadow got to the door, put a key in the lock, and unlocked the door.

It was Lace. She walked through the door, and I must have been holding my breath, as I breathed a heavy sigh of relief.

"What the hell were you doing back there?" I screamed.

"I pulled your car around back. We can transfer the body," Lace responded.

"Why the fuck are we using my car," I asked clearly irritated.

"I am the last person he was seen with. If I'm considered a suspect, my car will surely be examined. You don't even know this guy. No one will think to check your car," Lace concluded

Lace's response soothed my irritation. She was right, and it made perfect sense.

Lace apparently was upstairs planning next moves while we were wrapping up his body. Lace laid out the details of her newly developed plan, and we sprang into action. Lace had driven my car up as close as she could to the back door. She handed us each a pair of medical-grade gloves before we did anything else. Lace then provided us with more garbage bags which we laid right outside the door. She then poured some cleaning solution on the bags. The three of us walked back into the basement where the body laid and carried him out the back door. We lifted Carlos' body over the threshold and placed him on top of the flattened bags. We tore open the bags Jen and I initially wrapped Carlos in and Lace poured more cleaning solution and bleach over the body and the bags.

We hadn't worn gloves when we originally placed Carlos in the bags, so more than likely, our fingerprints were everywhere, and we didn't know if anything that could point this murder back to us lingered on Carlos. We hoped the cleaning solution and bleach would take care of that.

While we let the solution dry, we layered garbage bags in my trunk and taped them down the sides. We must have layered at least 20 bags in the trunk, taping them on top of one another and ensuring the trunk was completely covered. Once we were done, we wrapped the body back up in the bags and taped it as tightly as we could.

We got Carlos' body in the trunk of the car, and we went back inside and headed upstairs. Mrs. Thompson still sat silently on the sofa. She looked up when we reached the top of the stairs.

"Stop there!" she said as she stood up and walked toward the kitchen and grabbed a few more garbage bags. Mrs. Thompson returned to the basement door and instructed us to strip. "Take everything off and put it in these bags. I'll take care of these bloody clothes and ensure they're never seen again. We did as we're told. Mrs. Thompson collected the bags which held our clothing, hugged each of us tightly, and said good night, as she exited Lace's house.

LACE

I locked the door behind Mrs. Thompson and triple-checked the sliding door and all the windows, ensuring everything was secure. The three of us walked upstairs wearing nothing but our bra and panties. We showered one by one but remained together in the bathroom, discussing the rest of the plan.

"We'll dump the body on Friday night. The Burba Lake recreation park is the perfect place. Most of the events in that area happen Monday – Friday and during the daytime. If we stay away from the Burba Cottage, which is rented for nightly events, we should be fine. The base traffic will be light, and the area is dissolute. You guys will drive directly behind me, following closely. We'll pull up to one of the sites and toss him in the lake," I concluded.

Jen had some concerns about the body beginning to smell over the next two days, but since the temperatures were still rather cool, Nika and I didn't think it would be an issue. We agreed to not worry about it since it was only for one more day, technically.

After we were done discussing dumping the body, I was exhausted. Of course, not just from the conversation but all the events from the day. It takes a lot of energy to beat a man damn near to death. I still had to work in the morning, so we headed downstairs to the pullout, put on fresh sheets, and went straight to bed. I'm almost positive I was asleep when my head hit the pillow.

The next morning, I awoke and prepared for work as usual. Jen and Nika were up but not moving just yet. I showered, got dressed, and headed for work. I made it a point to arrive on time for daily muster. I wanted all my time to be accounted for.

After muster, I made my way to my desk and tried to act as normal as possible, but on the inside, I was a complete wreck. I couldn't concentrate and couldn't keep my mind from running wild. I kept imagining military police busting into my office and snatching me out of my chair, throwing me on the floor and handcuffing my hands behind my back, hauling me off down the corridor for everyone to see, locking me up under the jail, and never to be seen or heard from again.

I had to shake that thought from my head and tried hard to control the anxiety happening on the inside. I emailed Carlos as I normally would in the morning. He didn't respond to my first email so around lunchtime, I sent him another message. Of course, I knew he wouldn't answer that one either, but I wanted to stay on routine.

Around one o'clock in the afternoon when I hadn't heard from Carlos, I walked across the hall to see if he made it in, but really, it was just to make sure folks knew I was looking for him. Although we worked in the same building and right across the hall from each other, I didn't have access to where Carlos worked. He had access to programs to which I wasn't privy. Therefore, I didn't have free range in his spaces. I rang the buzzer and waited patiently for someone to let me in.

I pulled the door open after hearing the buzzer and walked in. "Can I help you, Petty Officer Miles?" some random soldier asked before I could get completely inside of the office.

"I'm looking for Sargent Hendricks. Is he in today?" I asked.

"Sargent Hendricks is on leave for the next two weeks. I think he drove home to see his family in Cleveland," the random soldier explained.

"That's right!" I said with a height of excitement in my voice. "I totally forgot," I mentioned as I turned and walked out of the office.

I went straight to the bathroom. I walked into one of the stalls and started dancing. I was so excited. I had totally forgotten Carlos was going home to surprise his mom for her birthday. That meant his mother wasn't expecting him and no one at work would be expecting to see him for weeks.

Hearing that news brought so much joy into my heart. I felt like God was shining a light down on me. I literally wanted to jump for joy in the stall, but I held my composure. I stayed in the stall for a little while dancing silently. Eventually, I went back to my office and worked the last two hours in bliss. I didn't let anything bother me, especially not the smart-ass remarks my stupid-ass supervisor made. I did make a mental note that my desire to kill my supervisor was increasing. Although I didn't pull the trigger with Carlos, I could definitely pull the trigger on this asshole. Except for that one thought, the rest of my day was pure joy. It was a complete breeze. I felt so relieved and I was too happy to let anything bother me.

Although my day was great and I was in a much better mood once I found out Carlos was on scheduled leave, my mind wasn't completely clear. I still needed to clean my basement, and I needed to do it fast. It also needed to be cleaned in a way where no one would ever suspect or find anything remotely close to evidence of a murder. Knowing that, after morning muster, I requested Friday and Monday off. I figured that would be enough time with help from Nika and Jen to get the basement in order.

I received my approved 96-hour liberty chit around 2:30 p.m. and when 3:00 p.m. hit, I couldn't get out of the building fast enough. I hightailed it out of there and headed straight home. When I arrived home, I noticed Sasha's car was in my parking spot. That made me smile. I wasn't expecting her until Friday night. I found a spot in the visitor parking lot and walked next door to Mrs. Thompson's house. I hadn't seen T since yesterday, and I wanted to check on him and Mrs. Thompson.

Mrs. Thompson and T were in the kitchen making cookies. T heard me call out his name and ran to me. I picked him up and held him tightly. I just stood there for a moment, holding and smelling him. I could feel Mrs. Thompson watching us. I walked over and included her in our embrace. We stood there together, exchanging no words. After a few long minutes, we finally released each other from our embrace. I put T down and soon as I did, he begged to stay. He didn't have to ask; he was staying anyway.

"Sasha got here not too long ago. I haven't been over, but they know I'm here if they need me," Mrs. Thompson said.

"I think we can handle it from here. I have tomorrow and Monday off, so hopefully, everything will be back to normal by Monday evening. Is it cool for T to say?" I asked.

Mrs. Thompson looked at me as if I spat in her face. "Of course! He is a child! What's wrong with you? Why would you even ask?" she responded.

I chuckled at how insulted she looked. "Thanks," I responded as I started to walk toward the door. I opened the door to leave when I heard Mrs. Thompson call my name, I turned to acknowledge her and she simply said, "Lace, honey, things will never be back to normal!" Sadly, I knew that was true.

SASHA

After speaking to Jen and Nika on the phone, I contemplated waiting until Friday to drive up to Maryland, but I felt like I needed to get there today that day. I called Robbie and told him I was going to pick Alisha up from school and then stop by the house to get some clothes for her for the weekend. I picked up Mason and called Mrs. Rodgers to ask if I could bring the kids over a day earlier.

They were young, it was okay for them to miss school on Friday. Mrs. Rodgers, of course, agreed and was more than excited. DD was there with no other kids and the company for her was welcomed. After getting all the kids situated and dropping them with Ms. Rodgers, I jumped on the highway and headed north.

While speaking to Jen and Nika, they suggested I stop and pick up several random items. I made the requested stops along the way to pick up the suggested, so it took me longer than expected to get to Lace's. I arrived at Lace's house in just over five hours. I parked and remained in the car for a moment. I said a silent prayer for protection and guidance, although, at this point, I knew God had our prayers in the do-not-answer pile. I got out of the car, leaving all the items I purchased behind. I walked up to the door and the energy just felt different. I knocked on the door and no one answered.

Lace had a doorbell but had taken the batteries out because it would often get triggered by the wind. The doorbell was heard throughout the house but knocking on the door did not have the same effect. I knocked on the door and waited a few more minutes before I called Jen. When Jen didn't answer, I called Nika, but neither of them answered the phone. "Where the fuck could they be and why aren't they answering?" I wondered.

I waited a few more minutes, and when no one appeared at the door, I went next door to Mrs. Thompson's house. She must have seen me coming. By the time I got to the door, she was there waiting with the door wide open. I hugged Mrs. Thompson tightly. We walked inside and sat in the kitchen.

Mr. Thompson was in his recliner in the living room, so Mrs. Thompson opted to sit in the kitchen. T came over and sat on my lap while we chatted for a while. I didn't mention anything about what had taken place at Lace's house. I didn't know if she had told her husband or if she wanted to discuss it while her husband was so close in proximity. I explained to Mrs. Thompson that I had knocked on Lace's door several times and no one had answered.

"They're probably downstairs in the basement cleaning and couldn't hear the door," Mrs. Thompson replied. She then reached on her key rack by the door and handed me Lace's spare key. "Thanks, I'll bring it right back after I unlock the door," I explained.

I ran back over to Lace's, unlocked the door, and took the key back like I said I would. Lace's house was creepy. I did not hear anything when I walked in. I stood on the inside for a minute and then became crippled with fear, and I screamed for Jen and Nika. It was a panicky scream. Fear was in my voice, and I heard it and felt it in my belly as I screamed. Nika and Jen came rushing up from the basement, looking terrified.

"What the fuck!!!" Jen screamed when she saw me.

"I don't know. You guys didn't answer the door or the phone and when I walked in, I didn't hear you guys. The distress in me took over, I guess that's why I screamed," I responded to Jen's unasked question.

Jen and Nika busted out laughing. I didn't find the shit funny at all.

"Help me with this shit in the car," I demanded over their laughter.

Jen and Nika ran upstairs to put on some clothes as they wore nothing but their panties, bra, and medical gloves. They continued to laugh as they were dressing and as they followed me out to the car. We made several trips back and forth to the car collecting all the items I was instructed to purchase.

Shortly after unloading all the items, I noticed Lace walking across the grass through the kitchen window. She looked like shit. I had spoken to Lace on Tuesday, and she told me she looked good, almost back to normal. Clearly, she didn't use an actual mirror. Lace still had deep bruises that I could see through the thick makeup she used to try and cover her face. She had dark circles under each of her eyes. She looked tired, defeated, and miserable. Lace entered the house, and I rushed to her and held her tightly. Lace cried silently while I held her. Eventually, she stopped crying, and I released her.

"Now that we are all here, what's the plan?" I asked. I was instructed to pick up a bunch of nonsense but had no idea why we needed half of the items I purchased. Jen and

Nika came up with a plan all by themselves while I was on the road, and Lace was at work. Jen and Nika first instructed us to strip down to our undergarments. "The less of our clothing we have to get rid of, the better," Nika announced. Nika and Jen then laid out the rest of the plan. It was a great plan: Lace and I both agreed.

I hadn't seen the basement. I had only heard how horrible it looked. Nika and Jen started the cleanup process with the cleaning supplies Lace had on hand, but apparently, it was still very bad and quite overwhelming. They cautioned me way too many times before we headed down.

I had the weakest stomach out of the four of us. Everyone knew it, which was why they tried to prepare me for what I was about to see. However, nothing could prepare my stomach for the massacre in front of me. As I walked down behind Lace and Nika, my stomach overwhelmed me, and by the time I reached the bottom step, I puked all over the floor. It was projectile vomit. I couldn't hold it or contain myself. I puked so much until only stomach bile came up. Jen grabbed me from behind and damn nearly carried me out of the basement, leaving a trail of vomit up each step.

I stumbled up to the third level and washed my face and rinsed my mouth. I stayed there for a moment, trying to get the sight out of my head. I was unsuccessful. The rest of the evening, I spent it gathering supplies and transferring items from the main level to the basement, and never going back downstairs. At some point, I ordered food, but we all agreed to eat once they were done for the evening.

It was around midnight when they came up. I had a bag near the basement door. As they came out of the basement each of them placed their gloves and the little bit of clothing they wore in the bag. They each went upstairs and showered while I heated up the food, fixed plates, and poured wine. They made their way downstairs as they were finished. We all sat at the table and ate silently.

Lace hadn't slept in her room since the incident. I finished eating first and went to shower upstairs. Once the others were finished, they pulled out the sofa bed and climbed in just as we had done the previous week. As we were drifting off to sleep, Lace began to speak softly, "Carlos' command thinks he's on leave. He was supposed to drive home and surprise his mom, so she's not expecting him either. I guess I didn't jump the gun."

I was so fucking annoyed by Lace's comment. I tried to keep quiet, but I just blurted out: "Shut the fuck up, Lace! The fuck you mean you didn't jump the gun? This wasn't the fucking plan. Now everyone is jumping through hoops, and you're trying to justify your actions? Get the fuck out of here with that bullshit. You didn't think about anyone but yourself when you jumped the gun!"

"Chill out, Sasha," Nika explained. "A lot was happening, and you do not know what was going through her mind or what it feels like to be in her shoes. So, chill!" Nika concluded.

Nika was right. So, I apologized to Lace immediately, but I had to admit I was frustrated. "Everyone had to drop what they were doing to get up here. We all have kids, families, and jobs." While contemplating saying that, I heard Jen whisper, "Tomorrow, with all of us cleaning, we'll be done in the basement, and it should be ready for the contractors to come in and do whatever they need to do; then we'll dump the body and this ordeal will be done and over with." I jumped up instantly, "What the fuck do you mean tomorrow we dump the body? Where the fuck is the body?" I questioned.

Nika sat up and softly said, "He's in my trunk, in the back yard. Now go to sleep, we have a busy day tomorrow." I stared at Nika in disbelief. Then I looked at each of them as they lay down in peace as if nothing had happened at all. As if a rapist had not been killed and was now in the backyard waiting to go to his final resting place.

Within minutes, everyone was asleep except me. My soul was uneasy, and sleep evaded me. I would doze off here and there, but soon as I realized I had dozed off, I would wake myself. At one point throughout the night, I got out of the bed and checked the doors and windows repeatedly.

I paced the floor for quite some time, thinking, "What the hell have we gotten ourselves into?" I found myself watching over my friends, my chosen sisters, diligently. "How would we recover from this? Would we ever be the same? Could we ever recover and be the same again?"

CHAPTER 8
NIKA

When I woke up, Sasha was already out of bed. She was in the kitchen, and she watched me intensely as I moved toward her. I could tell something was bothering her. There was a look of dread on her face that I had never seen before.

"I'm making coffee; you want a cup?" she asked.

"Sure," I responded, as I entered the kitchen and sat at the table.

"Lace found Antoinette's ring at Carlos' house when she went to drop off his stuff. She also found her gun and some other random female items," I continued.

As the words left my lips, Sasha turned around to acknowledge me talking and dropped the mug she was holding in her hand.

"Oh my God! It's the same guy," Sasha acknowledged with a huge smile. It's crazy how important it was for it to be the same guy for Sasha to be at peace with what we had done.

Sasha grabbed the mop, broom, and dustpan and cleaned up the mess from the broken mug. Then poured us each a cup of coffee while we waited for Jen and Lace to wake up. We sat there waiting for over 20 minutes before Sasha suggested we head downstairs and start cleaning. Luckily, we got most of the blood up yesterday, so Sasha was able to stomach it today. Sasha and I cleaned industriously in silence.

I had a lot on my mind, and I could tell Sasha did, too. With everything going on around me, I still was unable to shake Lamar out of my mind. I had such a great time with him during our lunch outings earlier this week and each time intensified my desire to be close to him.

Jen and Lace finally awoke and met us downstairs. Jen brought down a radio with a CD player and popped in a CD. The music started, and we cleaned, danced, and sang until there wasn't a visible trace of a crime scene in the basement.

We then opened all the windows and the basement door. We used a power washer Sasha brought up with her and power-washed every inch of the basement with bleach and a power wash cleaning solution and allowed the basement to air dry.

By that time, it was a little after seven, perfect timing for us to start getting ready to head toward the base. We all donned on our Navy-issued coveralls and discussed the plan one more time. Since Sasha was here, it was decided that Lace and I would ride together in my car and Jen and Sasha would drive Sasha's car behind us.

Lace and I headed for my car, which was still parked in the backyard, and Jen and Sasha headed for Sasha's car, which was parked out at the frontage. Lace drove as she knew exactly where we were headed. She drove around the frontage to ensure the others were behind us and led the way to the base. Sasha drove closely behind Lace to ensure no one got in between us.

It was a 20-minute ride to the base. As we reached the Reece Rd gate, we showed the guard our military IDs and were granted access. Sasha and Jen followed suit and entered directly behind us. We hit left on Ernie Pyle and left on Llewellyn Ave. It was pitch black. There wasn't a streetlight in sight. The road was lit by the midnight sun. After driving on the curvy road, Lace made a left on Wilson Street and a quick right on a non-identified road.

Lace backed in as close as she could possibly get to the dock and Sasha did the same. I looked at Sasha and Jen through the window to the right of me and Lace to the left.

"Are we ready, ladies?" I asked.

Surprisingly, everyone smiled.

"Let's do this, bitches!" Jen exclaimed as she busted out laughing.

That's what Jen usually did. If she got nervous, she laughed hysterically. We sat patiently and waited for Jen's laughter to subside, as we didn't want to draw any attention to ourselves. We took this time to put on our gloves and check our surrounding areas. There was absolutely no one around. It was a perfect spot to dump him. It took a few minutes, but Jen finally calmed down. We each got out of the car and walked around to the trunk.

We all tried to position ourselves on the dock, but the dock wasn't that wide, and we were so close to the edge of the lake I slipped. Jen grabbed me before I fell in. We wanted Lace to pull the vehicle up, but she insisted on staying where she was parked to make sure the body went into the water and did not land on the edge of the lake or under the dock. We tried to get the body out without meeting our own fate and failed miserably. So, Lace finally decided to move the car up just enough to keep us from falling into the lake. Once she did that, Lace and I took one end, and Sasha and Jen took the other end of the body. The body was wrapped so tightly there was no way for us to know who had the head and who had the feet. We walked to the very end of the dock.

"We'll swing and toss on three," I announced.

The count of three sounded good in my head, but the body was so heavy. It was so heavy it was slipping from both ends. We put the body down and took a breather. This time as soon as we picked the body up, I started counting. I didn't know if we could make it to three. We swung on my count and on three we all let go. The body made a huge splash, but no one was around to hear it. Once we heard the splash, we all rushed back to our respective cars and headed for the liquor store on base. We didn't need anything really but that was the excuse we would use for coming on base, just in case someone asked. Lace went in and purchased a couple of bottles of wine while the rest of us waited in the car.

We drove back to Lace's in silence. I felt such a huge relief when we arrived back at the house. I stripped soon as I walked in as well as everyone else. I grabbed our coveralls and put them in the washer machine in the basement. By the time I came back up, Jen had started the music, and everyone was dancing around in their underwear. I joined right in and we danced and drank wine until the wee hours of the night. The rest of the night was a complete blur. At some point, we all passed out in a drunken state.

Since most of the blood was concentrated at the bottom of the stairs, Jen had the idea to paint the basement floor black. No real reason other than just to erase whatever traces were left. We all agreed and spent Saturday painting the floor. It took a full day to dry even with all the doors and windows open.

The next day, late afternoon, after brunch, Jen, Sasha, and I headed back to VA, ready and willing to leave Maryland behind us. After dropping Jen off, I headed home, but I could feel something wasn't right. I shook it off because if anything would have happened, Lace would have called us by now. I called Jen once I parked to tell her that I made it home. When she didn't answer, I called Sasha. She too had just made it home. I wondered what took her so long to get home, but I didn't bother asking.

I got DD out of the car, and we walked into the house. I still had that weird feeling over me, but again, I shook it off. I didn't see Jay when I entered the house and that was a relief. As I passed by our bedroom to put DD down to sleep, I noticed Jay was passed out on the bed. Our bedroom reeked of alcohol. I quietly passed by and put DD in her bed.

I didn't want to wake Jay, so I opted to sleep on the sofa. I couldn't have been asleep for more than an hour when I was awoken by Jay, snatching me off the sofa and throwing me onto the coffee table. I hit the table and fell onto the floor. Jay got on top of me and began banging my head against the floor, yelling and screaming: "What time did I tell you to be home?"

I never answered his question because it didn't matter. It would have only made him more upset. Jay finally stopped banging my head on the floor and started choking the life out of me while he shoved his dick inside my pussy. My eyes widened as he shoved his dick in me. Jay had both hands around my neck as I tried to breathe. He thrust himself repeatedly. Jay's hands tightened around my neck tighter and tighter as he began to climax. My eyes rolled in the back of my head. As I was losing consciousness, Jay released his hands. I started coughing, trying to catch my breath while Jay stayed straddled over me, watching me struggle. When I was done coughing, Jay punched me so hard he knocked the wind out of me. Jay got up, pulled his pants up, and spat in my face as he walked away, yelling "Stupid bitch!"

I guess I should have expected some type of retaliation when I arrived home. I told Jay I would be home by early afternoon, but I got home much later than that. "Sometimes, I bring this shit upon myself," I thought as I cried myself to sleep.

JEN

The ride home felt quick! Not that I was ready to get home to the foolishness I was living with, but I was ready to get back to something normal. It was unrealistic how eerily calm we all were. I worried about Sasha taking the drive home by herself, but we stayed close behind her until after we picked up the kids. Then Sasha headed toward Suffolk, and we headed toward Virginia Beach for Nika to drop me off.

Robbie wasn't home when I arrived, and I was so thankful. I had no desire to deal with his stupid ass. I gave

Alisha a bath and then a snack before reading her a book and putting her to bed.

Once she was sound asleep, I went to my neighbor Josh's house, a few doors down, to buy some weed. I was in no rush to get home, so we sat on his balcony and smoked something out of his stash. Josh and I were cool. He's constantly flirting with me, every chance he got, and I shot him down every chance I got. It was almost like a game and entertainment for me and sometimes, I just felt like I needed the attention.

Josh was handsome, very handsome and buff just like I liked them, but we were neighbors and there are just some lines one doesn't cross. Josh and I always had great conversations, too. I believe it was by his design to wear me down. He would talk in the most calming and enticing way. I think he thought eventually that would do the trick, but he was just too close to comfort for me, and he was a thug-ass white boy. I don't do white boys or thugs! I like them a little rough around the edges, sure, but not a full-blown drug-dealing gun-toting thug!

While we smoked, I filled Josh in and told him about me walking in on Robbie fucking my section leader. He listened intently and then asked, "Is that the light-skinned chick with the big ass, or the dark-skinned one with the big tits?" I looked at Josh, and I was mortified.

"What the fuck, Josh? You knew he was cheating on me?" I asked.

Josh looked at me rather confused, "I thought you guys had broken up. One of the two of them is always over there, and I literally only see you when you come over to buy weed. I thought you moved out. Robbie had introduced me to both of the females, so I assumed you two were no longer together," Josh explained.

I was flabbergasted. I had so many questions, and I shot them off one by one, and Josh answered each one of them without hesitation. I couldn't believe how foolish I was, not to know, and I became infuriated, but was I mad at myself or Robbie?

Josh sensed my tension and offered me a different type of weed. He called it a laced blunt. He said it would help me to relax. I didn't know exactly what a laced blunt was or what was in it, but I took it anyway. Whatever it was, it made me feel great and after the third puff, I was completely relaxed. I don't remember much after that third puff. I vaguely remember walking back to my apartment and waking up the next morning in my bed.

SASHA

I prayed the entire ride home. I couldn't believe what we had done. We were each raised better than this. I tried hard to push the entire weekend out of my head, but the basement scene stayed with me relentlessly. I could not get the image out of my head and each time I tried, it returned with a vengeance, and each time, I got sick to my stomach. It got so bad at one point I had to pull over to a gas station and play like I had to go to the bathroom, and I puked profusely. I didn't want Jen and Nika worried about me taking the drive back by myself, so I didn't mention anything when I came out of the restroom. Although they were both standing there looking at me, waiting for an explanation, I ignored them and went to the car to wait for them to come back. Once we got back to VA and parted ways, I had to stop several times on the side of the road to throw up. It took me forever to get home.

MRS. THOMPSON

We all agreed not to mention this again, but Jim and I had been married for over 30 years, surely there was no way I would be able to keep this from him. After brunch, I stayed around and helped Lace clean up, and left shortly after the girls left. I had planned on telling Jim what happened when I got back into the house, but I didn't get the chance to bring it up first. Jim sat in his recliner with Antoinette's ring on the coffee table in front of him.

"Where did you get this from?" Jim asked firmly.

I released a heavy sigh and spilled the beans. I told Jim everything and I mean every single detail. Tears swelled up in Jim's eyes. "Why didn't you tell me?" he asked frantically. "I could have helped," he continued. He wanted to go over to Lace's and check on her or make her come stay the night at our house, but I told him that I promised Lace I wouldn't say anything. And he had to keep it between us. Jim reluctantly agreed.

LACE

Sunday after church, Mrs. Thompson came over and made us brunch. While we ate, she ventured downstairs and looked around. She was rather impressed with our clean-up job. Although nothing was visible to the naked eye, I knew there was still a possibility for blood to be seen through certain techniques. That's why while at work the other Thursday, I called the contractors who had previously worked on my house, updating the kitchen and the bathrooms, to finish the basement. They had already given me a quote, so I sent them the requested funds via a bank transfer for the materials and scheduled them to come out and start the project. They were due to arrive Monday morning. I hadn't really budgeted for the new design of the basement, but it was something that had to be done and quickly.

The rest of the day, the five of us solidified our story, just in case we were ever asked. After we were done, we agreed to never discuss it or mention it again. "What's done is done!"

The girls got on the road to head for Virginia around three p.m. and Mrs. Thompson headed home shortly after. I was once again left with just me and T. I hadn't spent much time with him over the previous week, and I didn't want him to feel neglected in any way. I didn't feel like doing anything, considering my insides were upside down, so I built a teepee in the living room, and we chilled there the rest of the day, only leaving the teepee for food or bathroom breaks.

We fell asleep in the living room like I had done every day over the previous week. I woke up the next morning to a knock on the door and it was the contractors. I opened the door to greet the contractors, and they immediately apologized for waking me.

"Sorry for waking you, Lace. I called Carlos a couple of times to get the key from him or to see if he would be here to let us in," the contractor explained.

"No worries!" I responded. "Carlos is on leave, so I'll be around for most of the project," I concluded.

We chatted for a bit about the project. Then I took them downstairs and showed them around. No immediate looks of despair graced their face which was a good sign for me.

The contractors unloaded the truck and got to work immediately. I stuck around the entire day to make sure everything went as planned. The first day was complete with no hiccups. I was so excited. I felt a sense of relief come over me. It would only take them three days to finish the project, but I had to return to work tomorrow, so I asked Mr. Thompson to let them in the next two days and check in here and there. He agreed.

The basement was supposed to be complete by Wednesday but, of course, that did not happen. It took them almost two weeks to finish. Mainly because I changed the original plan from a simple recreation room to a one-bedroom apartment with its private entrance just in case I ever decided to rent it out. Nonetheless, when they were done, it was as gorgeous in real life as in my head.

I felt like this thing was finally getting behind me.

Now if only the fear of being home alone would go away.

CHAPTER 9
NIKA

I didn't sleep. I stayed up most of the night, contemplating my life, wondering where the strength came from for me to kill Carlos, but not Jay. Jay's gun was next to me in the bag on the floor all night. Why didn't I reach for it? It would have been the perfect setup.

Instead, I just lay there and let Jay rape and beat the shit out of me. Jay never considered it rape. I had only started considering it rape after the training I took at my command. Jay thought you couldn't rape your wife, since you were married. But it was rape, though I never said no, and I would never tell Jay it was rape, it was still rape.

It was 40 minutes before I would normally get up when I finally said fuck it and rolled off the sofa. I don't even remember getting on the sofa. Sometimes I think Jay beats my memory out of me, too. I looked through my bag and grabbed Jay's gun. I made my way to our bedroom with the gun in my hand pointed toward Jay as I walked toward his nightstand and placed the gun back where it belonged. I was quiet, as I didn't want to wake Jay. He would kill me if he knew I had it.

I tiptoed away from the nightstand and over to the closet. I stopped short at the mirror. I glanced at my reflection long and hard. I was glad I had decided to get up, the extra time was needed to make up my face and hide the bruises left behind after Jay's attack the previous night.

As I stared at the bruises on my neck, I kept thinking I should have just killed Jay in his sleep. "It's not too late," I thought. "With these bruises, I know for sure that I could get away with self-defense."

"Next time, get home on time and you won't have to look so fucked up...stupid bitch!" Jay snarled from the bed, startling me.

I didn't respond to Jay. Instead, I gathered my things to shower and went into the bathroom. The bruises on my neck were deeper than usual. "I don't think makeup will cover them. I'll just do my best," I thought. I showered, thinking about leaving Jay. I knew I wasn't strong enough to kill him. "I don't know what came over me with Carlos, but whatever it was, I need it in me for my own life." After showering, I dried off and put on my underwear and a crisp white t-shirt. I opted not to wear a bra. When Jay threw me into the coffee table, I hit my back and shoulder right on the edge. It was still very sore. A bra would only irritate it more. I then pulled my hair back into a tight bun. I had a lot of bruises to cover and I needed my hair out of the way to see them all.

I washed my face and started with a tanning moisturizer as a base. Of course, I used one that was much darker than my skin. Then I used a dark concealer on my face and a body concealer on my neck. Once I was done, I completed the process again. The make-up didn't cover up the deep bruises, but it hid what it could.

Once my makeup was complete, I went to wake DD to prepare her for her day. I finished dressing and made DD's snack bag for aftercare while I waited on Jay.

Mom pulled up shortly before we were ready to grab DD. My mom was great when it came to DD. To help keep the friction down between me and Jay, she would sometimes pick DD up so Jay and I would not have to detour. Jay hated detouring, although he wouldn't have to if he didn't feel the need to follow me into work.

Jay and I pulled out right after Mom and DD. He followed me as usual, once on base, we parted ways. The good part about me transferring soon was that Jay would no longer follow me into work. The bad part was I would no longer be able to see Lamar.

When I arrived at work, I passed through the quarterdeck and ran into my supervisor on the way to my desk. He did a double or triple take, not exactly sure which one it was. "AZ3, you look like shit! Your time is short, and all your duties have been reassigned. Why don't you call it a day and if you still look like that tomorrow, take tomorrow off too?" he suggested "Sure, PO1!" I responded. It was no secret that I was in an abusive domestic relationship. I never said a word, but my body spoke loudly for me.

Nevertheless, I was elated to be sent home. I needed the time off, if for nothing else, then to heal. I hadn't planned on taking leave in between my transfers. So, the time off was appreciated.

I wanted to find Lamar before I departed for the day, though. He texted me last Friday and over the weekend, but I didn't have a chance to really chat with him. I contemplated logging in to check my email and then decided against it. I took out my phone and sent Lamar a quick text, just to say hi and let him know I was done for the day and was heading out. Lamar responded immediately and decided to meet me at the car so we could chat for a minute.

Lamar and I had become good friends, almost best friends, but that title was reserved for my girls. Lamar arrived at the car with a huge smile on his face and his arms extended to hug me. His embrace was super tight, and I flinched as I was so sore from my incident the previous night.

"Sorry! I fell last night, and my back is a little sore," I offered as Lamar released me.

He looked me over fully as if he knew the truth. He didn't say anything, but I saw him looking at the marks I tried to hide. He didn't ask about them, he never would. He simply caressed my face, softly, silently, touching every bruise I tried to hide.

Once he was done taking note of my badly bruised face and neck, Lamar suggested we walk over to our new-found picnic spot by the water. Of course, I agreed. I figured walking over would give us even more time together, and I longed for more time with Lamar.

We walked side by side at a very slow pace, talking and laughing and enjoying each other's company. We talked about my weekend in Maryland, and I had to lie about the entire thing. I wondered what Lamar would think of me if he really knew the truth about me. "Not just that I'm a murder, but how much I think of him; how I long to be in his presence; how sometimes I fantasize about fucking him, being with him, wearing his skin; and how much of a coward I really am."

I also wondered if I could be happy with Lamar, not like feigned happiness when everyone was around, but happy when it was just us. I was confused about my friendship with Lamar. Though we're just friends, I had these thoughts and feelings that sometimes made me think I wanted more.

Lamar's hand brushed up against mine and pulled me out of my wandering thoughts. He walked so close to me, or maybe it was me to him, that our hands often brushed each other, and each time it did, fire zipped down my spine. My excitement about Lamar was insane.

I remembered when I felt that way about Jay. "Maybe Lamar is just like Jay. Maybe he beats his wife and treats her like shit, too." I wonder if he would ever spit in his wife's face.

We arrived at the park and found a spot right by the water. It was early, so no one else was there. I loved that. Lamar and I talked without interruption for hours. When I finally looked up, the park was full. I smiled at Lamar and asked, "Don't you have work to do?"

"It'll get done," he responded nonchalantly.

That's how he was about everything. Nothing was more important than what he was already doing. He gave his undivided attention to everything he did—that even included lunch, talks, and walks with me. I often wondered if he was that attentive to his wife, or was I and the time he spent with me a welcomed distraction?

Lamar and I stayed there for another three hours, never taking our eyes off each other. Acknowledging each word the other spoke. That was unusual for me. I talked to Jay often, but most of the time, he didn't respond. Often, I had to ask, "Did you hear me?" and Jay would look at me crazily and still not respond. So, I began to assume by him looking at me, recognizing I was speaking was a yes response. Jay was so different than Lamar. I often wondered how I ended up with Jay, "Was I so desperate and lonely at one point that I settled, or did I actually love him?"

The crazy part is that I do honestly remember happier times. I remember getting butterflies at the sight of Jay. I remember getting spikes of excitement down my spine and in my belly. I remember the days of a throbbing pussy at the mere thought of Jay. I remember wanting nothing more than to be one with him, to feel his skin on my skin. I remember those things. I'm just not sure if it was in my head or if it was my reality.

Lamar and I finally decided it was time to head back. We walked back to the command, slightly grazing each other's skin. He embraced me when we got to my car, but this time I didn't flinch. He opened my car door for me and said, "See you tomorrow!"

The thought of not seeing Lamar the following day crushed me. "I won't be in tomorrow," I explained. "PO1 gave me the day off!"

"Any big plans?" Lamar asked.

I didn't have anything planned, as a matter of fact. I was still going to get dressed and act like I was going to work. I didn't want Jay to know I was off then he would want to know my every move for the entire day and if there was any time that was unaccounted for, Jay would make me pay, and honestly, my body couldn't take any more of Jay's anger this week.

"No plans! I'll probably just hang out with Jen," I responded.

Lamar smiled and nodded, acknowledging my non-plans. We waved goodbye, and I drove away in utter bliss.

On my way home, I stopped by the commissary and grabbed a couple of items for the house then picked up DD and headed home. The house was a mess from the weekend, I assumed. I cleaned up and made Jay's favorite meal. Lamar made me so happy when we spent time together. My happiness frequently carried over at home regardless of Jay's evil ass.

Jay arrived home shortly after dinner was made. I made all our plates, and we sat and ate dinner silently. Well, almost silently. Jay, of course, had a few insults about my cooking but damn nearly licked the plate clean. "Hypocritical, ungrateful bastard," I thought. We finished dinner, I cleaned the kitchen and prayed that the night would remain peaceful.

Jay went to the living room and started playing video games. I was thankful his attention would be on something else that night.

I normally did DD's hair over the weekend, but since I was out of town, I decided to wash and braid it that evening. With Jay playing his games and me doing hair, the clock was winding down without any of Jay's temper tantrums. I silently thanked God for answering my prayer as I put DD to bed and prepared myself for bed, too.

The next morning, our morning routine took place as usual. Once Jay and I parted ways on the base, I drove off the base and headed for Jen's house. I let myself in through the patio door, which was never locked. There was no sign of Jen or Robbie there. Jen started her clinical the previous day and was trying to get the hang of her new schedule. She had evening clinical which started at three and ended at eleven.

After letting myself in, I made a pot of coffee. I was quite surprised there wasn't a pot made already. Jen usually drank at least three cups a day. I took my coffee to the living room, sat it on the side table and plopped down on the sofa, and got comfortable. I turned the TV on but made sure the volume was down. I was flipping through the channels when I felt my phone vibrating. I looked down and saw a "good morning" text from Lamar. I almost jumped out of my skin.

That was Lamar's first time ever texting me so early. Actually, that was Lamar's first time ever initiating a text conversation between us. I couldn't help but smile profusely. I wanted to scream in excitement, but I wasn't sure if I was there alone or if Jen or Robbie was there in the bedroom. Instead, I responded immediately with a simple "good morning".

"What the hell are you cheesing at?" Jen asked as she entered the house

I jumped, "O my God!" I screamed. "You scared me."

"You're in my house as I walked in and you're scared?" Jen asked

We both started laughing, "Yeah! I guess you have a point," I responded.

I purposely didn't answer Jen's questions. While Lamar and I texted back and forth for the next few hours, I made a point to keep a straight face and show no excitement. We talked about nothing at all but just having his attention even in the texts made me happy. Before I knew it, it was lunch, according to Lamar. Lamar mentioned he was going to the sandwich shop and offered to bring me a sandwich to Jen's so we could have lunch together.

My insides became warm with the thought of me and Lamar at Jen's. In an instant, I saw me naked, straddling Lamar on Jen's sofa. I shook that thought and remembered I couldn't risk Jen or anyone else knowing about Lamar. Jen was already side-eyeing me.   I didn't want to give her or anyone else the wrong idea. Not that Lamar and I were doing anything wrong, but perception is sometimes someone's reality.

Instead, I agreed to meet Lamar at our spot by the water. It was a beautiful day for lunch by the water, but then again, every day with Lamar was beautiful.

When I arrived and saw Lamar standing there, smiling, waiting for me, something inside me clicked and I wanted to believe it was me realizing that it was perfectly fine for Lamar to be my best friend. Since the title, clearly, can be shared. But I knew that wasn't the case. I knew there was more to my friendship with Lamar. I would never admit it, and I knew he would never admit it. "But how much more is it to this friendship that I am unwilling to admit, and does he feel the same?"

CHAPTER 10
SASHA

I had finally stopped seeing the image of Lace's basement covered in blood once I threw myself into the planning committee of Carter's coming home party. The thought of Carter returning soon also seemed to lessen my depression.

You would think we were welcoming home prisoners of war with the extravagant nonsense we had planned. Most of it was Evelyn's doing. She was a show-off and went overboard for everything.

I was however thankful she had decided to take the lead on the party. It was getting way too big for our townhouse. Evelyn was so efficient in party planning. Two weeks prior to the boat's arrival, she started hosting nightly meetings to ensure everything was perfect for our husbands' arrival.

I thought it was overkill until I found out that she had also reserved a train and several carnival rides, then I knew for sure it was overkill, but she had the requisite space, time, and money to do it.

I was responsible for desserts, drinks, and water toys for their Olympic-sized pool. With a pool that size, I wanted to ask why they didn't have dumb-ass water toys, but I didn't. I took my little to-do list and went on with my business.

It really didn't matter what Evelyn asked me to do, I was willing and happy to do it. Planning a welcome-home party for Carter took my mind off everything: my pain, Lace, Jen, and Nika's pain. Planning this party was the most normal thing I had done in weeks, and I desperately wanted and needed normalcy.

As the days trickled by, my anxiety calmed, and excitement rose within. I was like a kid counting down to the day of Carter's return. And when the day finally arrived, I was overjoyed.

It was like the first day of school. The night before, I laid out my clothes and Mason's for us to wear to meet Carter in the morning. I wanted to make sure I was extra sexy but still appropriate. I wore a pair of snug, distressed hip hugger capris that hugged me in all the perfect places. My blouse was a low-cut floral top that slightly flared at the bottom. My chest was bare, so I donned a necklace Carter brought me a few years past. It fell perfectly on my cleavage, which always drew Carter's attention to my small perky breasts. I knew we would be standing most of the day, so I wore a pair of wedge floral sandals that matched my shirt. My hair was pulled back into a messy bun, just the way Carter liked it. "It reminds me of the way I look after sex," he once said.

Mason and I arrived at the port around 11 a.m. in anticipation of Carter's arrival. Evelyn somehow found us in the crowd. She was there with her four kids. I envied Evelyn a little, not because of her material things. I didn't care about her big house, fancy car, or extravagant things. It was the ease of her being able to carry a child to full term and produce a little human I resented, just a little or maybe a lot. It seemed like every time her husband breathed on her, she became pregnant, and I wanted that. More importantly, I wanted to give Carter what he wanted.

Not that our life was lacking in any way, but it was something about having a miscarriage or multiple miscarriages that made me feel incomplete, or not good enough. Or maybe just not as good as Evelyn.

From afar, you could see the waves changing as the ship began to approach. The families and friends waiting were going crazy. There were musical screams flooding the air as the ship got closer and finally docked.

Evelyn's husband was in the first batch to be released from duty off the ship. Evelyn and her kids spotted him right away and ran to him. We stood looking in the crowd, waiting patiently. I didn't move from my designated spot as Carter and I had already discussed where I would stand upon his return. I watched the families as they greeted their loved ones, while I waited, and a sense of peace rushed over me. It was as if someone was comforting me, letting me know that everything would be alright. That I too would have the renewed joy someday soon.

I heard Carter yell our names before I saw him. I followed the sound of his voice and locked eyes with him. He was in front of us before I could even move. He kneeled and grabbed Mason then stood up and hugged us both as tightly as he could.

"It's so good to be home. I've missed you guys like crazy," he whispered in my ear.

The three of us wasted no time getting away from the ship. We didn't even bother speaking or saying our goodbyes to anyone. Carter and I found the car, and he loaded his stuff in and hopped in the driver seat, and started the ride home. It took us about an hour to get off base and by the time we hit the highway, Mason was fast asleep. I knew Mason would sleep most of the ride home and planned accordingly.

I grabbed the sheet that I purposely placed in the back seat out and draped it over the driver and passenger seat, making sure if Mason woke up, he couldn't see what was happening in the front seat. Once the sheet was secure, I reached over to the driver seat and started massaging Carter's dick through his pants. Carter looked at me and smiled.

"Sasha, you can't, not while I'm driving," Carter said with a hint of desire in his voice. "Relax!" I insisted.

I leaned over into Carter's lap, unzipped his pants, and slowly began sucking his dick. I missed the taste of his dick, too. It was seasoned just right on the outside with a hint of sweetness on the inside. I sucked Carter's dick until he came in my mouth. "Dessert for lunch," I thought as I swallowed his sweet cum.

I expected Carter to last a bit longer than he did, but I was kind of happy he didn't, I was eager to taste his insides and he was damn near losing control of the car on the road.

After I was done, I placed Carter's dick back into his pants and zipped him back up. I removed the sheet I placed as a divider and checked on Mason. He was still fast asleep.

Carter continued to the house with a smile on his face and a rock-hard dick. There was no need to make any stops, I had made sure I brought all of Carter's favorite things during the week. I didn't have anything else planned as I knew Carter just wanted a nice quiet evening at home with all his favorite things, me and Mason.

Carter started talking, trying to clear his mind to make his dick go soft. He talked the entire way home, telling me all about his deployment and port calls. I couldn't wait to see the pictures. Carter described some of the most beautiful places. He talked about the new friendships he built and how he couldn't wait for me to meet his "brothers". He loved and hated deployment, for obvious reasons.

I would say that was part of the Navy I missed. I separated from the Navy right after Carter and I got married. The friends I made on my first and last tour were all I had in the area. I hadn't really met anyone outside of the Navy since separating. I also never had an opportunity to travel the way he did.

We got home in a little over two hours. Traffic was insane. Carter played with Mason and caught up on all the 3-year-old nonsense he had missed while I cooked a meal fit for a king. When I was done, we ate together and enjoyed each other's company. After dinner, Carter bathed Mason, read him a story, and put him down for the evening while I cleaned the kitchen.

I heard Carter coming down the stairs, as I was finishing up the dishes. I was anticipating his soft touch when he walked up behind me and grabbed me aggressively. I jumped, almost frightened at the force he used. Carter spun me around and kissed me intensely as he moved me to the dining room table. My body was pierced with pleasure as I breathed him in.

I was barely on the table before Cater pushed me back and yanked my panties off. My ass was hanging off as I tried to steady myself before Carter released my lips and kneeled before me to face my throbbing pussy. He began massaging my clit with his tongue, and it felt good. Carter inserted three fingers in me while he French-kissed my pussy, teasing me relentlessly until my legs began to shake and my body became weak as I climaxed in his month.

I wanted to please Carter just the same, but he had other plans. He motioned for me to turn over right there on the dining room table, and I did as I was instructed. Carter kissed my ass multiple times before he began biting it softly. He kissed me up my back as he stood behind me, removing his pants. I could feel his breath on me as I panted and moaned. Carter leaned in close behind me and slid his hard dick in. I gasped. It felt like heaven, I was seeing stars and butterflies above me as my eyes rolled in the back of my head.

Carter moaned as he thrust against me. With every pump, I felt seven months' worth of tension leave his body and mine as our souls became one. Carter collapsed on top of me after he exploded within me. We lay there on the edge of the dining room table until we both gathered enough strength to go upstairs.

Carter and I made love and fucked countless times over the next four days. We re-familiarize ourselves with each other's bodies, exploring new adventures. It was perfect! My mind was clear, and I didn't think about anything else besides us. It was even better that I was ovulating and had a good feeling about conceiving during this time. I didn't bother Carter with the details. I kept that to myself.

The welcome-home party was scheduled five days after the ship's return home. That gave us all enough time to have our own private celebrations with our mates and family, and Carter and I took full advantage. We didn't leave the house for the entire five days.

I invited Lace, Jen, and Nika to the party, but Lace was in no mode to travel. I couldn't quite understand why since she was having such a difficult time staying in her house. I thought for sure she would want to get away. Lace had just gone through a tremendous ordeal, and it was showing.

Nika and Jen both agreed to show face at the party. Evelyn and the other wives were cool, but they were not my damn friends. Carter would be there, but I knew how he could get when he and his boys had a get-together outside of the boat. On the boat, there were roles everyone played: some supervisors and some employees. The relationships were professional and separated, but off the boat, everyone was friends and equals. That's not how the Navy portrays it or what they want you to believe but that's what it is.

On base, Officers and enlisted lived in the same communities; they were neighbors and best friends. Their kids played together and attended the same schools. Their children often slept over at one another's homes, while the parents hung out until the wee hours of the night.

I knew this cookout would be no different. Evelyn's husband, Jake, was an officer, a Captain to be exact. We all lived in the same community. They lived on the backside where the single-family homes were, and we lived on the side with the townhomes. Carter and Jake would often get together on the weekends with a few of the other guys who happened to be on the same boat and lived in the community and played basketball. That was when Evelyn and I became cool.

Carter dropped me off a little early at Evelyn's to help her set up. If Evelyn couldn't do anything else right, she damn sure knew how to throw a party. Everything was laid. I basically showed up early for shits and giggles. I helped where I could and drank wine and mingled with the other wives that showed up early until Jen and Nika arrived.

Carter pulled up shortly after Jen and Nika arrived. He walked over, spoke to my girls, kissed me passionately, and disappeared into the wind. Jen, Nika, and I were attached at the hip as always. We chatted up the other party goers for a while, rode the amusement rides, and went swimming. At some point, we all got hungry. I looked for Mason and Carter to fix both their plates while I fixed mine, but they were both in their own little worlds. I made my plate and found a seat next to the girls while we ate and chatted. At some point, we found our way to a spades table, and it was on and popping.

When Nika and I got on the table, we couldn't be stopped. Jen normally played with Lace, but since Lace decided not to come, Jen had to play with some random. Nika had just dealt us a "Boston" hand. I had 8 books by myself and Nika had 5 books. That was all the books in the deck, and we were ready to play it out. Right after I threw my first card down, I heard Carter yell my name.

"Sasha! Meet Marcus. He is the brother I told you about," Carter concluded. It felt like someone's hand knocked the wind out of me as I turned and investigated the face of Lace's Marcus. Nika and Jen couldn't believe it either. We were shocked. Nika said something slick out of her mouth, but I couldn't quite focus on her words at the moment. I was in utter disbelief.

Marcus knew who we were too and tried to introduce himself to us. Again, Nika stopped him in his tracks with something slick flowing off her tongue. Carter stood there looking quite disappointed as if he had no idea what was going on when in fact he did. I shared everything with Carter, even my friends' love-life dramas.

I felt compelled to call Lace, I think we all did, but considering what she had just gone through, we decided not to. We figured we would give it a couple of days and then fill her in later, once things had cooled down.

However, three weeks later and things still hadn't "cooled down". We still hadn't mentioned anything to Lace about Marcus being at the party or about him and Carter becoming such good friends. Nika thought it was best that she didn't know considering all things. Jen and I reluctantly agreed and decided to just let it be. I couldn't help but worry about her finding out though. Carter and Marcus had become damn nearly inseparable.

Marcus knew our stance, but that didn't stop him from trying to get Lace's information. We held the line, and I made sure Carter knew to do the same.

Eventually, Marcus got the hint and stopped asking. Once Lace started back traveling, then the responsibility was on me to just make sure Marcus was never around when Lace came to visit.

CHAPTER 11
JEN

Just about a month had passed, and I only had thirty days until I was completely out of the military. I was so excited to be getting out. The best decision I ever made was joining the Navy, and I was one hundred percent positive that my second-best decision would be getting out of the Navy.

I set up to start my internship the same day I started terminal leave to ensure I wouldn't be without a paycheck. Well, my terminal leave started on a Friday and my internship started the following Monday.

The first day wasn't that bad since class ended early. But every day after that was hell. Classes went the full length which created a very long day each day except weekends. It was hard for me to get used to it, considering I was so used to my short military days. We never worked more than 6 hours a day unless we were deployed.

My days were super long now. I'd drop Alisha at school, go to class, then come back home after class and try to get a quick nap before heading for my internship. Most days, I was successful, but some days were a complete flop.

I wouldn't arrive home from the nursing home until after midnight. The first few nights were bad. I went home and went straight to bed after a shower but lying in bed next to Robbie made me hate coming home.

A week or so after I started my internship, I began to see Josh regularly when I arrived home. Josh would be up, sitting on his balcony, watching me closely as I exited the car. His balcony faced the parking lot so I could see him when I parked. Some days he would speak, others he would just stare. The first few days, I ignored him. I knew he was trying to get my attention, and I liked it, but I remained unwavering.

About two weeks or so into this routine, one night after my shift, I randomly decided to go hang out with Josh instead of going home first. Josh had been working overtime to get the pussy. I didn't see Josh that often before

I started at the nursing home, but when I did see him, he made a point to flirt. As I got out of the car, I waved then yelled to Josh that I was coming over. He smiled and was too excited about my announcement.

Josh unlocked the door to let me in and walked back to the balcony. I followed behind and sat uncomfortably close to him. Much closer than I had ever been before. He instantly started flirting once I was seated.

"I got this for you, ma," he said as he handed me a laced blunt.

I took the laced blunt, which happened to be already lit, so clearly, it wasn't for me. Nonetheless, I took a puff. It had become my favorite drug of choice since I tried it a few weeks past. As I exhaled, I decided that I would give Josh the pussy. Well, at least let him taste it. I wasn't quite sure if I was going to let that happen that night or another day. I knew not to take more than three puffs if I wanted it to go down that day, though. "I want to be completely aware of what's going on if it goes down tonight," I said to myself.

Josh put his hand on my thigh as he had done in the past. Normally, I would move it immediately, but this time, I let it rest. I let him think he was leading the way as he kept moving his hand toward my pussy. I'm sure he felt the heat coming through my scrubs. I contemplated going inside but then something inside of me wanted to be seen. Josh grabbed my head and held it steady as he kissed me intently. I placed my hand on his dick to feel it hardening while we kissed.

As it hardened, I massaged it until it was fully hard. Then I yanked his dick out of his sweatpants and played with it while staring at Josh in between kisses. Josh was a white guy, sexy, no doubt, but his dick was pink. I wasn't sure if my mind was going to allow me to put a pick dick in my mouth. I pulled my mouth away from Josh and went for it anyway.

I wrapped my lips around the head of his dick and sucked lightly, running my tongue across his opening, gently. I stayed there teasing him until he couldn't take it anymore before I took his entire dick into my mouth. I felt it in the back of my throat, and I opened my mouth wider. Secretly wishing I had taken a throat lozenge before I started.

I sucked Josh's dick until he entered a state of euphoria. Then he came in my mouth, entirely too soon, making me thankful I didn't waste the lozenge. I spat out his disgusting cum as I stood up and removed my scrub bottoms. My pussy was sweaty from working all day, but Josh was the type of guy that liked sweaty pussy. He never said it, but I could tell.

I could see lights from cars parking in the parking lot. I also heard a few neighbors commenting, but I ignored them. They had no business out that time of night anyway. After Josh came, he jumped up and out of his pants and pushed me back into the house. I bumped into the wooden coffee table on my way in. Josh guided me as I sat on top of the table. He then kneeled before me and moved my panties to the side. Josh stared at my pussy for a while, probably debating his next course of action. I ignored his thoughts as I pushed his head into my pussy. Fuck his thoughts!

Josh French-kissed my pussy like it was his job, and he was damn good at it. I orgasmed continuously in his mouth. I didn't know if it was the blunt or if Josh was just that talented at satisfying women.

Josh moved me from the table to the floor and slid his hard dick inside me and fucked me slow and steady. When we were done, he rolled off me, and we lay there and finished our blunt.

It was something about those laced blunts that took me to another place. Not sure where I went mentally during those times, I just knew it was silent and peaceful.

After that night, Josh became a part of my nightly routine. That was the only time we could see each other. I went to class during the day and studied for my state boards during my mid-day break. Josh had some bullshit ass job; however, his main source of income was selling illicit drugs.

Before Josh, I had never done anything more than weed, but since the twenties are all about experimenting, I was open to trying more, and Josh indulged in my experimentation. I always had my pick of whatever I wanted whenever I wanted when Josh and I hooked up.

Josh and I became extremely comfortable in our relationship. Robbie knew what was up, but thought it was payback for his actions. I was so over Robbie; I didn't give a fuck what he thought. I was happy when he told me he got moved up on the deployment schedule. He mentioned something about somebody breaking a leg, I think. "Shit, I don't know." I stopped listening soon as I found out he was leaving. I didn't care to hear the details of why and how. I just needed the date.

With Robbie out of the picture for the next six to nine months, life was going to be great. I could feel it in my bones!

The only problem I foresaw was Axel. I met Axel a week into my internship, and we hit it off greatly. Axel was my work boo, and Josh was my round-the-way boo.

They were so different. Axel was a little rough around the edges but not a thug. He got into a little trouble when he was younger but had since been reformed. Axel didn't do any type of hard-core drugs either. He might hit a blunt here and there but for the most part, he was a clean dude. Axel could meet my emotional needs. He's a take-charge kind of guy. A guy that could see what he wanted and would go for it, but otherwise polite and calm. The sex was good with Axel, but I think more so because I quickly became emotionally invested. Axel was the type of guy I could see myself growing old with. He saw me like he'd searched for me his entire life and finally found me.

Josh on the other hand was my fuck buddy. He fucked me like it's his damn job. He's nasty with it, too. I loved that shit. I didn't see any type of future with me and

Josh; he was just something to do and someone to get high with.

Axel and Josh did not know about each other, but they're both aware of my situation with Robbie. They were also both aware that Robbie was leaving for deployment soon, and each was looking forward to spending more time with me, preferable overnight.

The months flew by and before I knew it, Robbie had departed for his deployment, and I was graduating and preparing to sit for my state exam. I knew I would be nervous before the test, so I made sure to see Josh beforehand. I planned to see him and hit a blunt a few times to relieve the stress on my shoulders. Josh had other plans. He wanted to taste my pussy, which he thought would be more relaxing. I agreed and let him. A good fuck and joint equaled a great combination for relaxation before the exam. I made sure to only take two hits and saved the rest of the blunt for later.

By the time I got to the testing site, I was so relaxed. I checked in at the front and slid into my testing seat. I sat down, and it felt like only minutes passed before I was finished. I don't know for sure, but when I was done, it looked like some folks were just getting settled.

Over the next six weeks, while I waited for my test results, my relationship with Josh and Axel flourished. Robbie was completely out of the picture in my mind, and I was elated and living the dream with two men who truly adored me. For the most part, I was able to split my time with the two of them without the other knowing.

But recently, Axel had been desiring more and more of my time. He started asking to stay the weekend instead of driving back home to North Carolina, but with Josh being so close to home, I didn't know if that would ever happen. Then the perfect opportunity presented itself when Josh announced that he would be heading up to New York to pick up a package the following weekend. I toned Josh out at some point as I thought to myself, "Life just couldn't get any better."

I made plans for Alisha to spend that weekend with Nika and DD and planned the perfect weekend at my place for me and Axel.

Friday after I got off from work, Axel followed closely behind me as I led the way home. Axel lived in a hotel nearby the nursing home during the week, so most days, I would just go to his hotel room a little before work, and we would fool around or do whatever, but it wasn't the same as having him all to myself for an entire weekend. The thought of spending uninterrupted time with Axel excited me and made me giddy at the same time.

When we arrived home, after putting Axel's bag away and running bath water, I made us both drinks. We went back to my bedroom, stripped naked, and entered the bathtub with drinks in hand. We sipped our drinks slowly as we talked in the tub. We stayed in the bathtub until we were both wrinkled. After finally bathing, we exited the tub, made our way to the bed, and fell asleep tangled in each other's arms. It was the best night of my life.

We spent Saturday in bed, fucking and making love, only exiting to eat and take bathroom breaks. It was a perfect day, entangled in bliss. I lay there, smiling, thinking about how happy I was and wondering if this would be my forever when I heard my sliding door open.

"Jen!" I heard someone yell.

"Oh shit!" I said as I recognized the voice and began to panic.

"Who is that?" Axel demanded.

"Jen, where are you?" Josh yelled again.

I could hear Josh moving throughout the house. It wouldn't be long before he made it to the bedroom.

I jumped off the bed, "Hide in the closet!" I demanded.

"The fuck wrong with you? I'm not hiding in no fucking closet," Axel snarled.

"He will fucking kill you, please just hide for me.... please?" I begged

Axel was furious but unsure of who was at the door and what he might be capable of, he did as I instructed. Soon as I closed the closet door, Josh walked through the bedroom door.

"Hey!" I said with a smile.

"Hey, you!" Josh responded as he walked over and kissed me passionately on my lips.

I was so nervous Axel would bust out the closet any minute. I led Josh out of the bedroom, out the back door, and up to his apartment. Josh never wanted to sleep at my place since I still shared it with Robbie; therefore, it took no effort for me to lead us out of harm's way.

I stayed the night with Josh, too scared to go back and face Axel. I was sure he had left shortly after Josh and I left. I was also sure he would probably never speak to me again.

I flickered my eyes as to the sun beaming. The blinds were up, and the sun shone right in my face. I turned over and saw that Josh was still fast asleep. I felt like shit for what I had done to Axel. I got out of the bed, got dressed, and grabbed three freshly rolled lace blunts sitting on Josh's nightstand. "He has plenty," I thought, "he won't miss these few." I went back downstairs to my apartment, and of course, Axel was gone. All his shit was, too. I guess I expected that but a part of me really wanted him to be there. I don't know what excuse I possibly would have given him, or maybe I would have just told him the truth.

I thought about calling Axel to offer him something, an apology, maybe? Instead, I sat on the sofa and fired up one of the freshly rolled blunts I had just taken from Josh.

####

"What the fuck is wrong with you, Jen? Wake up! Is this why you wanted me to watch Alisha? So you and your lil boyfriend can spend the weekend getting high? Wake the fuck up dammit!" Nika screamed

I heard Nika, and I tried to wake up. I didn't even know I had fallen asleep. Nika was furious. I could see it in her face, but I couldn't respond to any of her requests. I don't know why; I just couldn't answer her. I just stayed there seated on the sofa numb, unable to move or respond. I was able to move my eyes, though, and I watched Nika silently as she continued to bombard me with question after question. I saw her moving about the house first into my room before disappearing into Alisha's room. When she resurfaced, she had a fully packed bag of Alisha's clothes, I'm assuming.

"Jen, what the fuck?" Nika screamed again before eventually storming out of the house with Alisha and DD.

When I finally emerged from my stupor, it was almost 8 p.m. So, I texted Nika to tell her I was on the way to grab Alisha.

"Don't bother. You were on some shit today! They're already in bed. Just get her tomorrow," Nika's response read.

Nika was right, I was on some shit, but what? What could have been in the blunt to make me feel like that?

NIKA

I grabbed Alisha's bag as I helped the girls out of the car. DD, Alisha, and I walked into the house through the back door.

"Hey, girl!" I hollered as I noticed Jen sitting on the sofa.

Jen didn't respond.

I walked over to where Jen sat and noticed she was drooling, but her eyes were wide open, so she wasn't asleep. Her breathing was slow and shallow. I began to panic.

Then I realized I'd seen that look before. It had Jay written all over it.

I started shaking her and screaming, "What the fuck is wrong with you, Jen? Wake up! Get up!" I screamed.

Jen didn't move. I didn't know if she didn't want to or if she couldn't move. I walked to the linen closet and grabbed a towel and soaked it in cold water. I put it over her face, hoping it would bring her out of whatever trance she was in.

"Is this why you wanted me to watch Alisha? So, you and your lil boyfriend can spend the weekend getting high? What the fuck, Jen?" I screamed again to no avail.

I looked around to see what Jen had taken and found a half-smoked fucking blunt. A laced blunt, I'm sure. "I bet she doesn't even know what's in there," I thought.

The cold towel wasn't helping, and I couldn't stand the sight of Jen. I packed Alisha some fresh clothes and the girls, and I left her high ass right there.

I was furious as I walked out of Jen's house. I wanted to call Sasha, but the girls were in the car so I decided the phone call would have to wait for another time.

JEN

I tried to wrap my brain around what happened earlier in the day, but I just couldn't get my thoughts together to answer any of the probing questions.

I fell asleep sometime after texting Nika and woke up the next morning, feeling like shit. I went to class and dreaded the thought of going to work and facing Axel but calling out wasn't an option. As much as I didn't want to face Axel, I knew that I had to, so I decided to go straight to his hotel before work and get it over with.

I asked Chelsea to pick Alisha up from school which would give me extra time to stop by Axel's. Of course, she agreed. She was Alisha's sitter while I worked in the evenings, but she felt more like family.

I didn't know how Axel would react, or if he would react at all. "What if he's not willing to talk to me?" I pondered. "I wouldn't talk to me. Why did I expect him to talk to me?" I asked myself

My heart was beating faster the closer I got to the hotel and the more I thought about it. By the time I parked, it felt like my heart was about to jump out of my chest. I attempted a few breathing techniques when I parked but nothing worked. "Fuck it. What's the worst that could happen?" I thought.

I made my way to Axel's room. He made sure to get the same room week after week. I lifted my hand to knock on the door and the door swung open. I saw Axel walking away as I entered. He sat on the bed with his left leg fully extended and relaxed and his right leg still planted on the floor. He leaned back on the headboard and stared me down. He just sat there staring in silence. I didn't know what to do so I just started talking.

"I'm sorry, Axel. I should have been honest with you!" was all I actually remember saying before Axel eventually cut me off.

"Who the fuck was that, Jen? And what type of nigga do you think I am to hide in a fucking closet?" Axel demanded.

I stood there and told Axel everything about Josh, the drugs; the fucking; the gun-toting; the laced blunts... everything, and I didn't even know why I mentioned any of those, but I did.

Axel interrupted me again and simply asked: "What do you want, Jen: me or Josh?" I answered before I even considered the question, "I want you, Axel!" I exclaimed.

Axel offered his forgiveness after I agreed to break things off with Josh for good! I couldn't believe it. I was shocked it was that easy, but happy, nonetheless.

I went to work in total bliss, but also a little nervous. My shift went by so fast, probably because I wanted it to go slower. I didn't want to break things off with Josh, but I had already given my word.

I drove home slowly thinking about my promise to Axel and my friendship with Josh. Above all things, we were friends, and I didn't want to lose our friendship.

When I arrived home, I noticed more cars than usual, especially for a Monday night and something felt off. Josh wasn't on the balcony like he usually was and there were no empty parking spots. I drove to the front of the building and found a spot near the other side. As I was walking to my apartment, I saw a man in the bushes waving to me to get inside and motioning for me to hurry up and be quiet. I ignored him. Then my apartment door open and the sitter started doing the same. "What the fuck is going on?" I thought. I ran inside and closed the door behind me.

"What's happening, Chelsea?" I asked.

"I don't know! A cop dropped this bag off and told me to tell you to put it in the closet and don't say a word or leave the house. Then seconds later, another cop came and told me to stay inside and don't come out. Then I saw cops knocking on all the doors, telling the neighbors the same," Chelsea explained.

As Chelsea was speaking, we started hearing loud bangs as if someone was knocking down a door or something and then scuffling. We both ran to the window to see what was going on and within minutes, the place was swarming with cop cars, and Josh was being escorted down the stairs in handcuffs.

I was mortified. Something inside me brought my attention back to the bag that was left for me to put in the closet. I opened it and saw Josh's drugs. An entire bag full of drugs and a stash of cash.

"Chelsea, who left this? Did you look inside?" I asked

Chelsea assured me she hadn't looked inside and again informed me that a cop dropped it off.

"Why would a cop bring me a bag of drugs and money to put in my closet?"

CHAPTER 12
MRS. THOMPSON

It's been over three months, and Lace has slept here every night. We loved having her and T with us, but Jim and I were worried that she's not recovering the way she should. Not that we knew how one should recover after being raped, but knowing Lace, I expected her to bounce back quicker than anyone else.

"Be as strong as Antoinette was after her rape. Antoinette rose hell. She didn't sit back, she didn't hide, and she wasn't ashamed. She fought back," I said one night while pacing the floor.

"And then she was murdered," Jim austerely reminded me. Jim lived to give me reality checks, no matter how hard or cold they were.

"Lace is strong, and she will recover. She will get through this, and she'll live to tell about it," Jim assured me.

"I think the media presence and the pressure from the cops are getting to her, Jim, and I'm really worried about her," I explained.

"If they had something on Lace, they would have arrested her by now. Shit, we all would be in jail. They haven't even found the body, you're worried about nothing, honey," Jim concluded.

Maybe Jim was right. Although we were both surprised that the body hadn't been found. I never asked Lace for the details of where they dumped Carlos' body. I assumed the less I knew, the better.

LACE

I didn't want to, but Mr. and Mrs. Thompson urged me to get counseling. They thought I was going through some type of depression. The truth was, I was just fucking scared, and I was so ashamed. The thought of talking to a stranger about what happened to me made me sick to my stomach, but after not being able to sleep in my own home for months, I decided to give it a try.

I chose to go to a civilian counselor, one out in the town, and I paid for it out of pocket. I didn't want my command knowing I was seeking mental help. I mean with a Top-Secret clearance, it's kind of frowned upon to need mental help. Although, the military branches would beg to differ, as they openly encouraged it. Sadly, those individuals leading the encouragement campaign were so high up the chain they didn't have a clue what went on day-to-day at the command levels. The backlash that came from your senior leaders if they dared to find out you were "seeking help" wasn't worth the help sought.

I started out seeing my counselor of choice every other week to start with, and as I got more comfortable, I realized I needed more help than I thought. So, after about a month and a half, I changed my frequency to once a week on Thursday evenings since T stayed with the Thompsons Thursday nights. Before I knew it, I was spilling the beans to Cynthia, my counselor. I told her about the rape, which was why I sought help in the first place. She listened to every detail intently. Cynthia would often look at me with pity in her eyes, and every week, she made the same comment. "It's not too late to go to the cops, Lace," she would diligently remind me.

I told Cynthia the same story I had told Carlos. "I don't remember the incident. I remember letting my random out around midnight, locking the door, and going to bed. I can't remember anything after that," I nonchalantly recounted.

Cynthia didn't believe me, though. One evening, she flat out told me so, "I think you know more than what you are telling me, Lace. I can't help you if you're not honest."

I wanted desperately for Cynthia to believe me, but she didn't, so I deflected. "I think I am just distracted!" I exclaimed

As much as I wanted to tell Cynthia the truth, I couldn't chance it. No one could know that Carlos raped me. His face had been all over the news and the cops suspected foul play. My supervisor was all too eager to inform law enforcement that the last time he saw Carlos was with me.

"What has you so distracted?" Cynthia asked.

"My friend is missing. He's not just my friend. He's like a brother to me and the cops suspect me!" I cried out.

"The cops questioned me three different times, totaling 27 hours and my story has never changed. But they don't believe me, and I don't know why. I would never hurt my brother," I mumbled through sobs. I looked up slightly, full of tears in my eyes to make sure Cynthia was immersed in my story and continued. "They spoke to my neighbors, too. Some of my neighbors said that they were sure that they had seen Carlos' car at my house the night he supposedly drove home to see his mom. I explained that Carlos had been there and left around 9-ish. My neighbors, Mr. and Mrs. Thompson, validated Carlos' time of departure. But the cops still just don't believe it, and I'm scared!" I cried out while continuing. "After a search of Carlos' house, the cops came back to me with a search warrant to search my house, I just can't believe they would treat me like that," I concluded in full-blown tears.

"Oh no, Lacey! I'm so sorry you have to go through that on top of everything else you are going through," Cynthia offered.

Cynthia ended our session for the evening after a few minutes of me sobbing. I was grateful. I didn't want to overdo it and give myself and my lies away.

On the way home from my session, I thought about a career in acting, especially considering the show I put on when the cops came to my house to execute their search warrant. I acted so surprised when they showed up, considering how close Carlos and I were. Apparently, the cops had heard differently. Although Carlos was nice to me in my face, he had made some unfavorable comments about me behind my back. Another blow.

The cops had also heard that Carlos had a reputation for befriending females and taking advantage of them once he had them in a vulnerable state. The cops thought this information and the information they heard from my supervisor were enough motives for me to want to hurt Carlos.

When the search began, I thought about informing the cops of where they would find blood. I had replaced all the carpet upstairs and on the stairs. I had also purchased a new bedroom set and new mattress and box spring. But I hadn't replaced the carpet in the foyer and living room, and I knew that my leap from the steps to the floor left a trail, but I also knew it was only my blood since there wasn't a scratch on Carlos when I saw him the day I returned to work.

All Carlos' blood had been framed out, dry-walled, plastered, and painted over for sure in the basement. But I didn't mention it. I let them do their search, and when they found blood right where I knew they would, they were all too happy. They just knew they had a slam dunk case.

"Ms. Miles, we have blood here. Any idea where this is from?" the lady cop asked.

I hadn't mentioned that I was raped, but I knew my supervisor had. "I was attacked," I responded. "I either ran or leaped over the steps, be it to get away from my attacker. I must have hit my head on the table before passing out on the way down," I announced as I loosened my bun and parted my hair to show the deep cut that recently heeled.

"Oh yes, we heard about that. Did you report that incident?" the male cop asked.

"No, I didn't. I don't remember much about the incident or who did it," I concluded.

I could tell neither of them believed me, but I didn't give a fuck. The cops concluded their search after coming up empty-handed as shit.

"We're going to test this blood we found to make sure it doesn't belong to anyone else," the lady cop announced as she walked away.

"Be my guest!" I offered with a smile.

They were looking for something very specific. A box of some sort, I overheard one of the officers say.

####

Surprisingly, my next session with Cynthia was great. Talking to her regularly was indeed helping, maybe not in the way she wanted to help, but helping me, nonetheless. Talking about the situation with Cynthia made me feel differently like it wasn't really me that was raped. Like I was just telling her a story about someone else. Anyone else but me. I'm not sure if that's how counseling is supposed to work, but it was working for me that way.

I started feeling better about myself, too. More like the old Lace. The Lace that needed to be out and free. The Lace that needed a weekend with her girls! But first, the old Lace needed to sleep in her own house, without fear.

On the way home from my session with Cynthia, I decided that that night would be the night that I slept at home, and if I could do it that night, I knew for sure I was doing better. I pulled into my parking spot, and I saw the light on next door. I was sure they were up waiting for me. I went over and just as I thought, my neighbor's parents were sitting in the living room, waiting for me. They had already put T down to sleep.

"I'm going to go home tonight and sleep there," I announced.

"Are you sure? You know you can stay here as long as you like," Mr. Thompson broadcasted.

"I know, but I think it's time," I said with a half-smile.

Yes, I was still scared, but it had been long enough, and I knew for sure Carlos wasn't coming back. So, what did I really have to fear?

NIKA

When I finally got around to calling Sasha, to tell her about Jen and her fucking foolishness, it was Friday. I meant to call earlier in the week, but Lamar and I had spent most of my free time together, "working late" and by the time I got home, it was usually too late to call her. Jay had a thing about me talking on the phone in the house, so I just didn't do it if he was around.

Soon as Sasha picked up the phone, the story just flew out of my mouth.

"She was literally sprawled over the sofa high as fuck. Drooling and shit like a fucking zombie. She literally couldn't move, Sasha!" I explained.

"I just don't believe it. When did she start this shit?" Sasha asked.

"I don't know, but it must have something to do with that new guy she's dating, Axel. He wasn't even there when I got there. He probably got her high and just left her there," I concluded.

Sasha was in utter disbelief, as was I. We decided that we would talk to Jen about this in person. Lace called the previous day and said she would be coming down that weekend. We figured this would be the perfect time to have a strong conversation with Jen. It wasn't my first-time seeing Jen high, but this was different. This was the start of an addiction.

And after being married to Jay, I know exactly what addiction looks like.

Although I missed Lace and desperately wanted to see her, her arrival time was smack dead in the center of my and Lamar's time. And with-it being Friday, I wouldn't see him for three days, if I missed seeing him that day. That would be the longest we'd ever gone without seeing each other. The thought of that made me sad, so I made a point to see Lamar and spend just a little extra time with him.

SASHA

Lace gave such short notice about coming down. I had to move a couple of things around to ensure Marcus wasn't around, while Lace was here. She hardly decided beforehand where she'd be staying. Lace would usually let the spirit move her, or so she would usually say. Nika wasn't allowed to have overnight guests, so her place was never in the running. It was usually between my house, Jen's house, or one of her favorites in the area. I was pretty sure staying with one of her "favorites" was out of the running since Lace hadn't had sex since she was attacked. She seemed to be doing better, but she wasn't fully back yet. Either way, I was so looking forward to seeing her, Nika, and Jen. I had great news to share with them, and I had waited long enough.

Lace shot past my house on the highway and headed straight for Jen's. She called me on the way and asked that I meet them there. Of course, I agreed. I hung up the phone only to notice Carter watching me, smiling. "What are you smiling at?" I asked with a smile of my own.

"You! I can't believe you have hidden this all this time. You know they are going to be mad," Carter concluded.

"I'll just tell them so much was going on that I forgot to mention it," I responded with a chuckle.

Carter had a full belly-busting laugh. "Forgot to mention it, huh? OK! Let's see how well that goes over with your crew," he said through his chuckles.

I purposely waited around the house a bit longer before I left. Nika had called and said she was running late, and I wanted to make sure everyone had arrived by the time I got there.

Although we had no plans to go out that night, and we were just going to sit around and talk, I decided to wear something to accentuate my figure and my baby bump. By now, I was surely showing, and I couldn't wait for the girls to see.

I arrived at Jen's and noticed everyone's car was there. I got Mason out of the car, and I began to get nervous. I don't know why the nervousness came about, as I was super excited to share my news with my friends. As I walked to the patio door, Mason shot past me and ran into the house. I could hear other kids playing as I got closer, and I smiled, thinking of my new bundle of joy joining the ranks of them. I walked through slowly, twirling, and smiling.

"Oh my God!" Nika screamed. "When the fuck did that happen?" she questioned.

Nika noticed me before anyone else. Lace and Jen damn nearly jumped out of their skin when they heard Nika. After they figured out what was going on, they all ran to me, hugging and rubbing on my belly. They were so excited, and so was I. I became so overwhelmed with excitement that I started to cry.

"Damn hormones," I said through giggles.

"I am so happy for you, Sasha!" Lace exclaimed.

"Me too," Jen chimed in.

"We have to celebrate!" Nika yelled as she walked to the fridge and pulled out a bottle of wine and Welch's fruit juice, the peach flavor. The exact fruit juice I drink when I'm pregnant. As a matter of fact, it was the only fruit juice I drank when I was pregnant. Nika brought the juice over and sat it in front of me with a smile on her face.

"You assholes fucking knew?" I asked.

And in unison, they all answered, "We sure did! You can't hide anything from us." "Who goes on alcohol cleanse during the summer?" Jen asked

"Pregnant people," Nika responded.

And then they laughed.

It was a night full of laughter.

Jen told us the story of hiding Axel in the closet because one of her randoms popped up. We laughed so hard. We couldn't believe Axel hid in the closet. Lace laughed so much she snorted. It was so good to hear Lace laugh again. At one point during the night, I thought back to the last time I heard her laugh, and I couldn't remember.

Her laugh was infectious. It filled the room and it was missed.

JEN

"I didn't know what else to do but ask him to hide," I said through my own laughter.

"How did he look when you let him out the closet?" Lace asked through a belly-busting laugh. Normally, I wouldn't engage when I knew Lace was making fun of a situation, but Lace hadn't laughed in months and it was good to hear her laugh, so I indulged. I thought she would never laugh again. And I was glad I was wrong.

I didn't tell the complete truth, but I did share with the girls the funny part. I didn't want them to know about

Josh. They hated him, just from the small interactions they had with him. Instead, I told them it was some random I met that had only been here one time and found his way back. I got rid of the random quickly, then Axel and I spent the rest of the evening smoking and fucking. Plus, it wasn't their business whom I was fucking.

NIKA

Sasha and I gave each other side eyes while we listened to Jen's story. Jen tried to make it seem innocent. As if the blunt she and Axel smoked was just weed, but I knew the fucking truth. She was making all sorts of excuses for this motherfucker. She tried to make him seem like a good guy. "Good guys don't give you laced blunts," I thought as I rolled my eyes. I wanted to say something, but Sasha kept slightly kicking me, motioning for me to stay quiet. I remained silent, but that didn't stop me from a continuous eye roll though.

We still hadn't told Lace about finding Jen high as fuck. And Lace was in such a good mood, finally, laughing again. So, I let the blissful moments ride, and Sasha and I agreed it'd be best to wait until the next day or Sunday to have a three-on-one with Jen. Since that night was clearly reserved for laughs that we all needed and obviously missed. It was late by the time all the laughing stopped.

I left DD with the other kids and headed home with thoughts of my and Lamar's earlier outing on my mind. The thoughts were so intense. By the time I reached home, I had been engulfed in my thoughts of him that my fingers found their way down to my pussy. I imagined Lamar sitting on the passenger side taking note of the arch in my back, and slight perspiration on my skin as he watched me bring myself to ecstasy as my fingers circled around my clit.

Once I exploded in my driver seat, my reality sat in. I dreaded entering the house. I must have been holding my breath when I entered as I breathed a heavy sigh once I realized Jay wasn't home. I undressed quickly, showered, and went to bed.

By morning, Jay still hadn't returned. It wasn't unusual for a payday, so I hurried and got myself together and headed back for Jen's.

Saturday morning was easy-peasy as we all decided to stay over by Jen's. The last time we all stayed together was the weekend we spent cleaning up Lace's mess. This was a welcome change. The next morning, I made breakfast and we sat around and talked.

Jen was beet red and angry as hell as she listened to me tell Lace about finding her high as hell. Sasha had already heard the story and wasn't surprised at all. Lace on the other hand was shocked as fuck. I just stared at Jen and shook my damn head, while she tried to blame her actions on Robbie, saying she just needed something to take the edge off. It was all overload for Lace, I had forgotten that we hadn't told her about Jen walking in on Robbie. So much had happened over the past few months, we had somehow forgotten to mention them. Well, it was really Jen's story to tell. She probably forgot because she was too busy getting high with the new loser in her life. Jen had it so good, I couldn't understand why she would let some lowlife try and bring her down.

"I think you need to leave him alone, Jen," Sasha announced strongly.

It wasn't a question or a request, and Jen knew it wasn't. I agreed with Sasha's thoughts, but of course, I couldn't and wouldn't dare verbalize giving relationship advice. Lace loudly also demanded that she should stop seeing him and then looked at me to say something.

"I agree with both of them," I said softly. I spoke softly because I knew Jen could give a fuck less about what I thought. And the look on her face solidified my thoughts.

Lace wanted to get on the road before it got late, so she gathered her things and prepared to leave shortly after breakfast. We all said our goodbyes and separately headed out, but not before making Jen promise and pinky swear to ditch the loser, Axel.

Jen reluctantly agreed, but it was something about the way she agreed that made me think she was full of shit! The look on her face or maybe it was her nonchalant demeanor that just didn't sit right with me.

As I drove home, I shook the thought off. Considering my situation, relationship advice was the last thing I had to offer.

CHAPTER 13
SASHA

I drove home from Jen's feeling quite uneasy. It was something about that pinky promise that just didn't sit right with me. Jen was holding something back, but I couldn't quite put my finger on it. With this pregnancy and my emotions, I wasn't sure if something was off with her or me.

JEN

"The fucking audacity!" I thought as I listened to Nika's judgmental ass. "Who the fuck did she think she was? Out of all of them to have something to say, she should be the very last one to talk," I thought silently as I listened with anger.

I listened to them demand that I stop seeing Axel and even pinky swear to it, but I had no intention to stop seeing Axel. "He isn't even the problem, but Ms. Judge all thinks she knows everything." I didn't even attempt to correct them. I just let them think what they wanted to as I hugged them all goodbye as they left.

I laughed within as I watched them pull off. Axel could partake in weed but that's about it. He's a straight-up guy. He didn't even like when I smoked laced blunts. He hated it. I never did it when he's around. Well, I tried not to, but sometimes I picked up the wrong blunt. It's easy to do.

Since the house was finally quiet, I put Alisha down for a nap. I went into my closet and pulled out the bag that Josh left for me. I still hadn't heard from Josh or the cop that dropped it off. I often went inside and took whatever I needed. I didn't touch the money though. I never took money from Josh; drugs I took from him all the time, mostly weed, so I knew he wouldn't mind.

Some days, especially a day like that day, l needed something a little stronger than weed. I grabbed some weed and mixed it with some other shit he had in his bag. I still hadn't learned what was in a laced blunt, so I just made it up as I went along. Most days, I got it close to right. Since Alisha was napping, I decided to take more than my typical three puffs, and it felt good.

At some point, I was awoken by Alisha, screaming and hollering. I didn't know how long Alisha had been there trying to get my attention, but the sun had already set by the time I woke up.

LACE

As I drove back to Maryland, I thought about how much I had missed over the past few months. I had been so wrapped up in my own shit, I hadn't paid much attention to my friends. I didn't even know Sasha was pregnant. Nika and Jen told me when I arrived at Jen's house Friday night. I felt completely out of the loop. As if life was passing me by.

I needed to get myself together, but I didn't know how to. Yes, talking to Cynthia helped but it wasn't the fix I needed. I needed something else but didn't know what.

This weekend was great and made me feel like I needed my girls on a regular basis to get back to being myself. I didn't know for sure, but maybe seeing them more often would help.

I knew for sure I needed to be more present with Jen. I didn't know what she's going through that would allow her to entertain a relationship with a drug addict. Just so unlike her.

I decided to spend the next couple of weekends in VA, and it was clearly the best decision ever. With the holidays approaching, I opted not to go home as I figured Mom would know something was off. Instead, I lied to her and told her Sasha was having a difficult pregnancy, and I wanted to help see her through it.

It wasn't a total lie. Sasha wasn't sick but mentally she wasn't herself. She was so nervous and scared of losing the baby she didn't want to do much of anything. So, I went down almost every weekend to help her out. Nika was there, too, and we planned Sasha's shower to help get her mind off the stresses of the pregnancy. She had become so tense lately.

We hadn't seen much of Jen since our talk, but being a new nurse working shitty and long hours, her free time was limited.

SASHA

Over the course of the year, Carter and Marcus' relationship grew, which naturally caused my relationship with Marcus' fiancé, Alysa, to grow. She was a doll and very fond of Lace. Alysa often asked why Lace was never around or why we hadn't all hung out since Marcus' return from deployment. Most of the time, I was able to change the subject quickly. I didn't want to make up a lie, because they were so hard to keep up with.

But now Lace was killing me, coming down every weekend. I couldn't change the subject quickly enough with all of Alysa's questions. So, I just stopped talking to Alysa altogether. Plus, Lace would have killed me if she knew I was friends with Marcus and his soon-to-be wife. Lace didn't stay with us every weekend, but just to be on the safer side, I made sure that Carter only hung out with Marcus at their place. I didn't want any accidents. Keeping Lace and Marcus apart was more stressful than the pregnancy.

Once I made it into the third trimester, I felt relieved almost as if I had made it. The fear of a miscarriage simply diminished almost instantly. Everything was going smoothly, and I just knew the upcoming year was going to be great.

Nika and Lace planned my baby shower, although since I was having another boy, I really didn't need one. It was more of an excuse to have a party, I thought. Carter had spoken to Marcus and told him the situation. Marcus knew he wasn't welcome when Lace was around, but he didn't want Alysa to feel any type of way. So, Marcus came up with an excuse to take Alysa away for the weekend. I was so thankful Marcus was understanding, and over time, I could see why Lace felt for him.

The shower was a hit. Everyone we knew showed up. My parents even came up for the occasion and surprisingly, Mom was on her best behavior. Strangely, whenever I was pregnant, Mom was much nicer to me. One would think she actually liked me.

Lace and Nika put their hearts and soul into it, planning and executing the shower. Jen hadn't been a part of the planning committee since she was working so many hours, but I did expect her to be at the shower. Instead, Jen was a no-call-no-show, and I knew immediately something was wrong. I didn't care how many hours she worked, Jen would never miss something so important and something in my belly just didn't sit right. I made a mental note to keep my thoughts to myself and take a trip over to Jen's once Lace headed back home.

Over the next few days while home, bored and on bed rest, I called Jen several times, but she didn't answer. I knew damn well she wasn't working around the clock. I was sick of being in the house and decided to sneak out once Carter went to work.

I got myself into the shower and felt a few slight pains in my side, but it was nothing to write home about, so I continued on my mission. Once dressed, I got in the car and headed for Jen's. I arrived at Jen's shortly after 11 a.m. It was just right around lunchtime. As I pulled up, the pains in my side got worse. I wasn't sure if it was anxiety or the baby. I had no reason to be anxious, so I chalked it up to the pregnancy and made a mental note to go straight home after I visited Jen.

Jen's sliding back door was open, as always. I walked in and yelled her name a few times and no answer.

I knew she had to be home since her car was in her parking spot, but there was no sign of her. I checked Alisha's room and Jen's room and still nothing.

As I was heading out, a sharp pain hit my side, and I felt the immediate urge to go to the bathroom. As I walked toward the bathroom, I heard a strange sound coming from that area—almost the sound of snoring. I walked in slowly, not to startle anyone, and there she was, fully clothed, sleeping in the bathtub, snoring. I took a deep breath and screamed her name to the top of my lungs: "Jennifer! Get your ass up!" and as loud as I was, she barely moved. She opened her eyes and turned to face me. She was high as fuck. I became so angry. I wanted to fucking slap her. I felt my heart palpitate, and I felt my blood heat and warm. And pee gushed out between my legs. My fucking water had broken.

I screamed again for Jen to help me, and she couldn't fucking move. She just lay there high as fuck, stuck in the bathtub, fully fucking clothed, staring at me like a zombie.

I was so nervous and scared. Not sure whom I was more scared for more. I wanted to call for help, but I couldn't let anyone see Jen like that. She would lose her license, and I didn't want to be responsible for that. As I stood there contemplating my next move, Jen's phone rang. I answered it and spoke softly. Tears began to flow when I heard Nika's voice on the other end. She was yelling something about finally answering and I softly cried: "Please come help me!"

NIKA

I rushed into the house and grabbed Sasha. I didn't even bother checking on Jen. I was fucking over her. I rushed Sasha to the hospital. I must have blown through every light. I was so nervous. Sasha was in so much pain. She called Carter to meet us at the hospital, and soon as she heard his voice, her voice cracked, and she broke into tears. I couldn't bear to witness it.

Carter somehow made it to the hospital before we did. I pulled up to the emergency drop-off area, and Carter and a hospital attendee ushered Sasha out of the car. I watched as they carefully placed her in a wheelchair before I drove off to find parking. I parked quickly and headed in. I called Sonya while I was walking in, but I had forgotten she was out doing workups in preparation for her deployment. I hurried inside and found my way to Sasha's room. I didn't want Sasha to go through this without at least one sister by her side. A few hours later, Sasha gave birth to a healthy baby boy. They named him Micha.

I was so ecstatic for Sasha and pissed as shit at Jen. There was a rush of emotions, so I instantly escaped to thoughts of Lamar. It had recently become the place I escaped to, away from reality.

SASHA

Micha's little face, fingers, and toes were all perfect. His skin, warm and soft. I was in love all over again. I couldn't have been happier.

Carter was happy, too. He fell in love all over again with Micha, Mason, and me. It was something about the way Carter looked at me. The love he had for me and our boys. He was so committed to our family, and I thanked God for him daily. My love for Carter grew daily almost like an obsession. I couldn't imagine living this life with anyone but Carter.

The first few weeks home with Micha were a breeze. He's such a good baby and slept most of the time. I wasn't as tired as I was when I had Mason. I felt a little more prepared this time around. Nevertheless, Mom and Dad still came up to "help". Well, their version of help, anyway. I really thought Mom just wanted to come home to be here for Sonya's workup return. Sonya had been out to sea back to back preparing for her upcoming deployment, and Mom was missing her talks with her baby girl.

It didn't take long for Mom's energy and true feelings to show their true colors. Three weeks into Mom's visit, I was ready for her to go. It's not that she had done anything wrong. She loved my boys, and she cared for them better than she ever had me. The problem was me. Well, not so much me but her hatred for me.

She tried to hide it, but it ran too deep and always reared its ugly head. I loved having Dad around, but I couldn't have one without the other. I contemplated sacrificing the time I spent with Dad just to get rid of her, but I couldn't stomach it.

Dad was aging, and I knew he wouldn't be around much longer. I wanted him to have as much time as he could with my kids. So, I tolerated all of Mom's bullshit, and when I couldn't tolerate her, I escaped somewhere quiet with Carter or Nika.

Jen's place would have been the ideal escape, but we weren't speaking. Well, I wasn't speaking to her. She'd been calling like crazy, but I was still upset and hurt by her actions and carelessness for her and Alisha.

I usually didn't hold grudges, but I couldn't get past the fear I felt, not only for myself but for Jen as well. "Why would she jeopardize so much for this Axel character?" I asked Nika during one of my get-aways from my mom. "What does he have over her?" I asked, perhaps rhetorically.

"Who knows?" Nika responded. We should get rid of his ass and get him out of the picture for good," Nika said with a chuckle.

"And how do you suggest we do that?" I pondered.

"I don't know. Fucking kill him, I guess," Nika responded with a hearty laugh.

I laughed too at Nika's extreme solution to the problem. But on the way home, I couldn't stop thinking about it. "Why not kill Axel? He won't be missed. He lives in a hotel during the week and with Jen on the weekend. When he travels home, he returns to an empty house. No one would think twice about not seeing him. It could be an overdose and then Jen would really see how bad these drugs are for her." I considered it the entire way home, and by the time I reached home, I realized it was my emotions getting the best of me. I would never want to cause Jen that type of pain, no matter how mad I was.

Once I got settled in the house, I decided to call Jen and put an end to my silent treatment.

"Sasha!" Jen answered with too much excitement in her voice. "I'm so glad you called. I'm so sorry I scared you. Please forgive me. I really want to meet Micha!" Jen blurted all at once.

"I forgive you!" I responded with a half-smile and a hint of attitude in my voice. "But, Jen, we have to get this under control!" I lectured.

Jen ignored my comment and went straight into catch-up mode. She wanted to know every single detail about baby Micha. Of course, I indulged and shared every little aspect of my bundle of joy. She interrupted me several times, apologizing profusely throughout the conversation for scaring me; and ensuring me that she had gotten her shit together. I ignored most of her comments and continued to talk. "Time will tell for sure," I thought silently. We talked for over an hour and by the end of the call, we had planned for her to come to meet Micha in person the following day.

I was excited about Jen's visit. I missed her, and I could tell she missed me, too. Not talking to her hurt both of us. And she felt some type of way about not meeting baby Micah, especially since both Lace and Nika had already met him. I think that hurt her more than intended, but it was her own fault, and I had to remember that. I would admit, though, I was quite excited for her to meet him. He was such an angel.

The rest of the evening was uneventful, just the way I had grown to love it. The next morning, after Carter departed for work, to my surprise, Mom and Dad headed out for breakfast alone. They didn't even ask if I was interested in going, not that I was, but it would have been nice if they had asked.

I thought it was rather cute the way they still dated one another. Although a part of me couldn't help but think it was Mom's way of keeping me and Dad apart. She hated our relationship. It didn't matter, though. Dad loved us both relentlessly, and he would do whatever he needed to ensure each of us knew that.

I think seeing the way my dad loved Mom was what made me fall in love with Carter. Carter demonstrated that same type of love for me on day one. It was as if he knew I would be his wife, and he knew exactly how to love me as such. Carter had mastered that. The love Carter and I have is equally rooted so deeply. It runs through our blood and gives us breath to breathe each morning. I'm sure that's the same love my dad has for my mom. My mom for my dad, not so much. She is different. Sometimes I feel like she is incapable to truly love someone.

While my parents were out, I prepared for Jen's visit. Although we caught up on the phone, there was nothing like being in each other's presence. I needed to see her and make sure what she was saying was in fact true. I tidied up a bit and dressed Micha in an onesie that Lace brought that read, "My mom is calm, but my TT's fight." I thought it was the cutest thing ever. Once I dressed Micha, I poured myself a glass of wine and waited patiently for Jen.

Jen was supposed to arrive sometime around nine a.m. after she dropped Alisha at day care, but it was now pushing noon. Mom and Dad had returned from their outing, and Jen still hadn't shown up. I called her several times, but she didn't answer.

Lately, not answering had become Jen's s thing, and normally, I wouldn't think anything of it, but that day, I had a bad feeling about it. Real bad, but I didn't want to think the worst. I phoned Nika and had her try to reach Jen. She too was unlucky. The feeling in my belly became overwhelming. Nika tried to calm me, but she too felt that something was off.

However, Jen had agreed to pick up DD and Nika was sure she wouldn't forget. So, Nika and I agreed to meet at Jen's around five p.m. I wanted to go right away, but Nika said she couldn't leave work until after five. That annoyed me since I knew Nika was in transition. I couldn't understand why we had to wait until after 5:00 p.m. I know what it's like to transition from duty station to duty station, and you never work full days during that time.

I ignored the thoughts about Nika since I already had Jen on my mind. I called her a few more times as I watched the clock intensely, still no answer.

Just as the clock struck 4:15 p.m., I was heading out, Sonya pulled up. I had totally forgotten that she was returning from her workups that day. She was overly excited to be back and meet her new nephew. She ran up to me, and we embraced tightly. I was happy she was back. I debated leaving Sonya with my parents and the kids while I went to check on Jen but decided not to. Sonya was deploying soon, and my nephew would be going back with my parents, so I opted to spend all the time I could with them before their departure. I called Nika and informed her that I wouldn't be able to make it to check on Jen. I asked her to go and make sure all was well, and of course, she agreed.

CHAPTER 14
JEN

Sasha still wasn't taking my calls. It'd been a few weeks already, and I still hadn't met baby Micha! Nika was still speaking to me, but a part of me felt like it's out of obligation or just trying to make me jealous. She and Lace had both met baby Micha. Nika had been telling me all about him. I hadn't spoken to Lace either; I'd avoided her judgmental ass. I knew I scared Sasha, and she had the right to be upset. I was trying to give her space, but she shouldn't be that damn upset and she shouldn't be punishing me by not allowing me to meet baby Micha either. It's just not fair.

"Why don't you just pop up over there, as she does you?" Axel suggested.

"I would, but Sasha's parents are in town and her mom is funny. She acts as fuck. She can barely stand Sasha. Let alone us," I explained.

"Well, if you want to meet the baby that bad, just go. I don't understand what the big deal is anyway," Axel continued.

Axel didn't quite understand my relationship with my friends. They weren't just friends to me. They're my family. They're really the only family I had besides Alisha. He didn't get that. Axel was an only child, so he didn't feel like he was missing anything. I had siblings, a mom and a dad that didn't want me and didn't acknowledge my existence, so I longed to have the relationship I built with my friends. He also couldn't grasp why a parent wouldn't like their child, especially if the child was Sasha. She was damn near perfect. It was unbelievable how anyone couldn't love her.

As I was trying desperately to explain it to Axel, my phone rang. It was Sasha, and I was ecstatic and relieved. Axel was draining me.

I don't think I let Sasha get a word in if it wasn't about baby Micha. Nothing else she said mattered. I just wanted to know every detail. This was my first time not being there when one of our kids was born. I felt like shit. I felt like I had missed out on so much, even though he was just a few weeks old.

Sasha and I talked for over an hour and made plans for me to meet Micha the next morning. I was overjoyed. I wanted to celebrate my type of way, but Axel was there, and he was a buzz killer, so I opted not to. Instead, I made dinner for Axel and Alisha, and we watched a movie. An uneventful evening, just as I had grown to love.

"Jen, what the fuck is this?" Axel yelled, shaking me out of my sleep.

I looked toward Axel and saw him holding the black duffle bag that's been stashed away in my closet. I turned beet red. "Why the fuck are you in my closet?" I asked.

Not that it mattered, but I was trying anything to deflect the situation. I didn't want Axel to know that the bag belonged to Josh. He would think I was still dealing when Josh when the truth was, I hadn't even heard from Josh. Or the cop that left the damn bag.

Axel completely ignored my question and spat off questions after questions.

I got out of bed and headed for the bathroom. "Axel, I need to drop Alisha off, and then I'm going to Sasha's. We can discuss this when I return," I explained.

"No, we can't discuss it when you return. We're going to discuss this now!" Axel demanded as he grabbed my keys off the table and pocketed my cell phone.

I looked at Axel and laughed. "You can't be serious!" I yelled. "You know how long I've been waiting to see the baby. You're fucking crazy if you think you're going to hold me hostage until I give you answers to questions that are none of your damn business," I concluded.

"I'll take Alisha to school, and when I get back, I want this shit out of here!" he insisted as he stormed out of the house with Alisha in tow.

I rolled my eyes, thinking about how tired I was of everyone telling me what the fuck to do. I picked up the bag and placed it on the dining room table. I remembered rolling a laced blunt and throwing it in the bag for ready use later. I reached in and had to fumble around for a bit before finding it. It was partially crushed.

I straightened the blunt out a little and fired it up. I took a few drags, and before I knew it, Axel was back to ruin my buzz. The sound of his voice at that moment deeply annoyed my soul. He sounded just like the three musketeers: Nika, Sasha, and Lace.

I was so over him. I don't know how long he went on for, but it felt like hours. Talking about fucking nothing. I ignored most of his childish ass screams and cries. I just sat there, focused on my high, trying hard to appreciate the moment.

"Do you fucking hear me, Jen? I thought once I had that nigga locked up this shit would be over!" Axel screamed.

"What the fuck did you say?" I yelled as I jumped off the sofa. I instantly lost it and became overwhelmed with emotion. I began hyperventilating as I attempted to ramble off question after question: "You had Josh arrested? What the fuck is wrong with you? How could you do that? Do you know what will happen to me, to Alisha, if he found out?" I jabbered each question one after the other.

I don't know how much time had passed with me and Axel arguing. I was so hurt; I just couldn't believe he had called the cops on Josh. At some point, I became so overwhelmed. I began to cry and went silent. We weren't getting anywhere yelling at the top of our lungs, and we weren't even listening to what the other had to say. When my crying finally subsided, I spoke softly: "Axel, let's try to talk this out, without yelling and screaming," I suggested.

The air became quiet and thick. Axel stared at me forcefully with anger in his eyes. "Please go ahead," I motioned toward Axel. I listened to Axel in hopes that he would hear me out as well.

As I stood there trying desperately to listen to Axel and understand his point of view, I became angry all over again, and my blood began to boil. I stayed silent as long as I could before I just snapped, and before you knew it, we were back to yelling and screaming to the top of our lungs at each other.

In the midst of our arguing, Nika came rushing in through the patio door with Alisha and DD in tow. I suddenly calmed down when I saw the look on the girls' faces. I had forgotten to pick up the girls, and Nika was fuming. I followed her gaze as her eyes focused on the bag full of drugs on the table. She started going off. But I couldn't even try to engage in conversation with her then.

"Nika, everything is cool. It's not what you think," I said calmly. Nika didn't even try to hear me. She was livid, and I could tell. "Nika, can we please talk about this later?" I suggested as I reached for Alisha. Nika snatched Alisha from me and stormed out, screaming some obscenities. I wanted to follow her and get Alisha, but I decided not to since I still had to deal with Axel and the bag of drugs.

Axel was still furious, but we had both calmed down significantly. He left the kitchen and sat on the sofa with his head in his hand. "What are you doing, Jen? This is crazy," he mumbled. Axel was right, I did need to get the drugs out of the house but couldn't just toss the drugs in the trash.

I hadn't heard from Josh, but I knew eventually he would come back for his drugs. I had recently found out that Josh's apartment was still his apartment. Someone was paying the bills, and it was empty. Seeing Axel looking defeated and hurt, I decided that I would just take the bag back up to Josh's apartment and hide it somewhere in there. With that thought, I went and sat next to Axel and assured him that I would have the drugs gone by the following day.

NIKA

I don't know how Lamar was able to skate out of work so often, but he did. We only saw each other during working hours so I was thankful that he was able to get away as often as he could. Spending time with Lamar had become a mental escape for me.

Our daily walks to the water had become so soothing. We walked so closely together, slightly grazing each other by accident on his part, I'm sure, but purposely on my end. I saw Sasha call, but I ignored it. The time I spent with Lamar was dedicated to just him since it was only a few hours a day.

"I'll call Sasha later," I thought as the phone rang again and again. "Answer it," Lamar said with a smile. He had such a gorgeous and inviting smile. His smile often made me smile and forget everything around me. My ringing phone brought me back to reality. I didn't want to answer it, but I did, and I immediately regretted it. Although Lamar and I only saw each other during working hours, it was very easy to extend working hours by an hour or three, and lately, Lamar and I had been doing just that.

But the urgency in Sasha's voice was telling me that would not be happening today. It was the same story of Jen. Everyone was so worried about fucking Jen, but Jen wasn't worried about Jen, and I was fucking over Jen. But Sasha was so deeply concerned. I tried to calm Sasha by informing her that Jen had agreed to pick up DD, and I was sure she would. I didn't tell Sasha that Jen had been picking up DD regularly and had never forgotten. Instead, I just assured

Sasha the best I could. Nonetheless, Sasha was determined to go over to Jens. I couldn't help but agree to meet her at Jen's shortly after 5 o'clock p.m.

As I hung up, I decided to ignore all the thoughts of Jen and Sasha, and stayed in the present moment with Lamar. Focusing, being with, or talking to Lamar was literally the only thing that made me feel normal.

Lamar noticed the change in my attitude. I was so disappointed at the thought of leaving him. I often wondered if he felt the same since he never showed any emotion. "What's wrong?" Lamar asked.

"That was Sasha. She wants me to meet her at Jen's," I said with a heavy sigh.

"Well, what's the problem? You love spending time with them, don't you?" Lamar questioned.

I looked at Lamar with a shy smile. "He was right. I loved my girls but getting to Jen's at 5 and dealing with her and Sasha was sure to make me late getting home. I didn't want to anger Jay, I thought. But I could never say that to Lamar.

I didn't answer Lamar, as I didn't know what might leave my lips. My thoughts and my words weren't coinciding lately. Instead, I changed the subject to talk about Lamar.

He never really liked talking about himself, but I loved hearing about his life as a boy. So, I'd often ask him questions to probe his memory and inspire conversation like, "Do you remember the first time you tasted ice cream?" He would go into deep thought and take a long sigh. If he was able to remember, he would smile and look at me deeply and start describing the moment exactly as he remembered it.

All his stories made me smile. They were such fond memories he carried. Lamar was so detailed and descriptive in his stories. I always felt as if I was in the exact time and place when he shared his stories with me. I imagined myself being side by side, watching young Lamar in his journeys through life. I learned so much about him during those times. I understood him more and developed a sense of gratitude and respect for him.

I wanted to think of Lamar as a brother, but the more time I spent with him, the more attracted to him I became. A part of me thought that I was making myself fall for him to forget everything going on around me. But my palpitating heart and throbbing pussy at the very thought of him knew different. Though I tried to deny it, I knew what was happening. I felt the lines of friendship blurring every single day. Still, I couldn't help but want to be in his presence.

While listening to Lamar and daydreaming about licking the ice-cream off his fingers as it dripped, I felt my phone buzz, bringing me out of his story. I had turned the ringer off to ensure I wasn't interrupted or so I thought. Lamar, always the gentleman and always so concerned, motioned for me to answer. I rolled my eyes when I saw Sasha's number again.

"Yes, Sasha!" I answered, clearly irritated.

"Hey! I forgot Sonya was getting back today, and she just pulled up. I'm going to spend some time with her since she leaves soon, so I can't meet you at Jen's," she concluded.

I didn't even think before I answered, "No problem. Enjoy your time with Sonya. I'll go by and call you later," I responded with a huge smile. I hung up before Sasha had a chance to say anything else.

"Good news?" Lamar asked with a smile.

"Kind of," I responded. "I don't need to rush off to meet Sasha anymore!" I concluded.

"Great! Because this story is nowhere near over," Lamar said as we both giggled.

Lamar and I sat out by the water for a couple more hours. Neither of us was in a rush to leave, but we had an unspoken agreement to always part ways by five p.m. Anytime spent after that would be considered inappropriate for sure, and neither of us wanted to give off the wrong impression. Though this day, I wanted to push the limits since it was a holiday weekend. I wouldn't see Lamar on Monday, so I wanted just a little extra time with him.

"Are you heading for Jen's now?" Lamar asked as I rolled my eyes. Lamar and I had discussed in detail how I felt about Jen and her bullshit. "Yea, I'm going to grab DD then head home," I responded.

Lamar smiled, leaned in, and hugged me tightly while whispering in my ear, "Get home safely!" Lamar's lips on my ear sent electricity down my spine, and my insides got warm as he held me a little too long, but not long enough. I wondered if he felt it, too, as he released me. He opened my car door, and we said our final goodbyes for the weekend.

As always, when Lamar and I departed, I was on cloud nine. I blasted my music and was heading straight over for Jen's when my phone rang again. I was sure it was Sasha, but I was wrong. It was Ms. Williams. I heard the young lady on the other end speak, "Alisha hasn't been picked up, and you're listed as an emergency contact!" she concluded.

"I'll be right there," I responded without thinking. I instantly hung up and called DD's school, hoping maybe Jen was just running late, but no, that wasn't the case. DD hadn't been picked up either. I was furious. I sped off to get DD, then rushed to get Alisha. On the way to Jen's house, I became more and more furious. "Like what the fuck is up with this chick?" I pondered.

I noticed Jen's and Axel's cars in the parking area. I parked in an open spot and got the kids out of the car. As I walked up to Jen's place, I could hear her yelling and screaming at someone. I rushed inside to see what was going on.

"What the fuck?" I said as I entered through the patio door. "I could hear you guys outside," I said as I noticed Axel. Before either of them could answer, I looked on the left and on the dining room table, and next to Alisha's highchair sat a black duffle bag. It was partially open, and I could see the contents inside. I instantly had a rush of emotions overtake me from fear to anger as I noticed Jen following my gaze.

"Nika, it's cool! It's not what you think," she adamantly stated.

"It's cool? Cool? What the fuck is cool about a duffle bag full of drugs sitting on your fucking dining table?" I looked at Axel and became disgusted. I looked back at Jen, and tears formed. "Is this what we're doing now? Really, Jen?" I asked sarcastically.

"Nika, I can't talk about this right now with you. Can I call you later?" Jen asked as she attempted to usher me out the door.

"Fuck you, Jen! I don't know what the fuck is going on, but I'm not leaving Alisha here with this bullshit," I stated as I yanked away from Jen.

Jen looked at me as if she wanted to speak, but instead, she was silent

I was fucking livid; I couldn't believe what was happening. I became overwhelmed with anger and stormed out of the house. I put the kids in the car and got in and sped off as tears ran down my face. I was so distraught. "What the fuck is Jen into?" I didn't want to call Sasha since I knew she was already worried. I would probably make things worse in this state. So, I called Lace.

CHAPTER 15
LACE

I was having difficulty maintaining a constant level: it was happiness or sadness. Some days, I felt like I was getting back to Lace, and other days, I felt like I was too far gone from who I once was. I couldn't find a balance. I didn't really enjoy the people around me anymore. I spent my time with T, and Mr. and Mrs. Thompson. I had no desire to hang out with anyone my age or anyone from work. The trust was gone. I couldn't trust anyone in Maryland except the Thompsons. I trusted them with everything. They were my family, and they needed me just as much as I needed them.

Mr. Thompson had fallen ill. They thought I didn't know, but I did. I'd seen it before in my own father. I didn't know what's wrong with him exactly, but I knew it's not good. I decided that I'd let them share the news with me when they were ready.

I continued to see Cynthia as I tried to find a balance in my emotions and perhaps a level of normalcy. The sad part was I didn't even know what normal was anymore. Was I supposed to revert to the same Lace that hung out all the time? I honestly didn't know what was expected of me. Was I now responsible for being an advocate to protect my younger sailors from future Carlos? What was my new normal and whose decision was it to make?

Honestly, I didn't want to be an advocate for positivity. I wanted women to respond just as I did. I wanted abused and rape victims to teach their abusers and rapists lessons after they were abused. My mind wasn't in the right space for advocacy or positivity. I was still healing my damn self.

But Cynthia wasn't here for it. She was Miss. "Old-goody two-shoe counselor". She was encouraging me to become an advocate. To speak out. "If you stay silent, he wins!" she would say.

I often wanted to laugh when she would say that. Carlos wasn't winning shit but a dead man floating contest.

I never told Cynthia that Carlos raped me, but I thought she figured it out. Although she never said it. She kept encouraging me to warn young servicewomen to be wary of whom they befriended. She would say that "most older servicemen don't mean younger servicewomen any well, and they should hear that from you". She spoke as though she had some experience with servicemen doing her wrong. Or maybe she had heard enough stories to know how common it was.

I wasn't sure if she knew or not. A part of me thought she did, but then the other part wasn't sure. Cynthia and I worked a lot on forgiving myself and coping through the loss of a dear friend. In this case, that dear friend was Carlos since he was still missing. I cried often when I spoke of Carlos, not because I missed him, but because he raped and betrayed me. The betrayal had become the most difficult thing for me to get over. Carlos and I were just friends. He was one of my best friends, or so I thought. The hurt that came from the betrayal was deeper than anything I had ever experienced or imagined and for that, I cried, and I cried often.

Most days, though still mentally bruised and broken, I felt better, emotionally and physically. I believed that was due to spending the holidays in Virginia. Now back in Maryland, I had been drowning in my own thoughts, and I hated it. I tried to find any and almost everything to trick my mind into happiness on those days; I struggled, but the only thing that seemed to work was being in the presence of my girls in VA. I was thankful for the long holiday weekends, especially the upcoming MLK weekend. I needed to get away, but I also felt the need for a more permanent move.

I wasn't up for orders for another nine months, but there were some hot fills open that I could take that would get me back to VA quickly, but doing that would shorten my shore duty and extend my sea duty. Wasn't quite sure if that was the move I wanted to make, but I knew I had to get the hell out of Maryland and back to VA.

Looking over the hot fill billets had become my favorite evening pass time. Not that any of them stood out to me. Just hoping that one would stand out. New ones were posted daily, and the quicker one applied, the better one's chances were of getting selected. The more I looked, the more I realized why they were hot fills. The choices were horrible and all of them were sea duty, particularly ships preparing for deployment. I wasn't interested in going straight out on a deployment. I needed a ship that had just come back from deployment. A ship that would be in the yards for some time.

The sound of my ringing phone pulled me from the deep thought of the newest hot fill that had been posted.

"Hello!" I answered a little irritated at the interruption.

"Lace!" Nika screamed through a cracked voice. "I just left Jen's house, and she's fucking lost it. I don't know what the fuck is going on, but they have a bag of drugs on the table. He's a fucking drug dealer, and he's storing the shit at Jen's house. That's why she's always fucking high. She gets the shit for free!" Nika concluded all without taking a breath.

I listened to Nika compellingly, but that didn't sound like the guy Jen had described to me. I wasn't particularly fond of Axel, but I didn't take him for a drug dealer either. He didn't seem to have that much ambition. From what I had gathered, he was a typical worker content with the bare minimum.

"Hold on! Sasha is calling," Nika abruptly announced. I sat on the phone waiting patiently for Nika to return, not really sure what to think of everything I was hearing.

"Lace, Sasha, you there?" Nika asked as she returned to the call.

In unison, Sasha and I responded. Nika then continued with her story as Sasha chimed in occasionally.

"It's bad, Lace. It's really bad," Sasha added. "Jen was supposed to be here this morning to meet Micha. Why would she miss the opportunity, considering how upset I was?" Sasha asked.

"I'm not sure, guys, but this just doesn't sound like the guy Jen told me about," I answered.

"We have to do something before she gets too far gone," Sasha continued.

"Lace, you haven't seen her in this state. It's bad. It's fucking horrible. Today she forgot to pick the girls up from school. She's not focused on anything but Axel and their damn drugs. She's two steps away from being an addict. Trust me, I know. I'm fucking married to one!" Nika concluded.

I was surprised to hear Nika announce that Jay was an addict. Although we all knew she had never acknowledged it. Jay had it bad, and I could see why Nika would be so concerned. "What do you suggest we do?" I asked. Before the question could fully leave my tongue, Nika and Sasha were already discussing a plan, and I was mortified.

"What the fuck is wrong with yall?" I screamed. "Why the fuck would we kill an innocent man? That's crazy, and yall have lost your minds!" I concluded.

"He's not innocent. Our friend and sister is in trouble, Lace. Are you above helping her?" Nika sarcastically asked.

"There are other options here, guys. Let's be reasonable," I suggested.

"That's funny... how there are other options for Jen, but there weren't other options for you, Lace!" Sasha exclaimed.

I started feeling like I was being attacked. I just couldn't get on board with this crazy-ass idea of theirs. I didn't know if I would have felt differently had I seen Jen in the state that they had. But I also didn't know how often Jen engaged in this habit and neither did they. "It could be recreational," I made the mistake of saying out loud.

"It's not!" Sasha and Nika responded in unison.

"Lace, we're doing this, this weekend with or without you!" Sasha announced.

"We were there for you in your time of need, and we expect the same in return!" Nika demanded.

I sat in silence, for I don't know how long. I felt trapped. I knew if I felt this strongly about getting rid of Axel, and I asked for their help, they would be onboard without a doubt. What was stopping me from getting on board? It's not like we hadn't gotten away with murder, so I knew it could be done. And clearly, he's not a "good guy". "We would probably be doing society a favor by getting rid of him," I thought silently.

"Are you in or out, Lace?" Nika asked, interrupting my thoughts.

"What's the plan?" I asked with a huge sigh.

The feeling to get back to VA intensified after my conversations with Nika and Sasha. I knew once we completed that task, Jen would really need us by her side. Especially if it all went according to plan. So, I applied to the hot fill at the National Security Group Activity that was just posted. It was a sea duty billet, but I would only be assigned to ships as needed, and I was almost certain my name wouldn't come up for deployment for at least a year after my arrival.

I wasn't sure that I would be selected, but I felt mighty good about it, considering I had all the qualifications and was willing to complete additional training.

MRS. THOMPSON

Jim had refused to keep his appointments even after I made them. "He won't get out of it today, though." I had taken off work to make sure he went to the doctor. He hadn't been feeling well, and he's getting weaker.

Thursday when T was over, Jim struggled to lift him. "That's unusual for Jim, considering how strong he is or how strong he used to be," I thought. "He's become fragile, and I know there's something wrong, no matter how much he denies it. He hasn't been himself for a while now."

"Jim, are you ready? Your appointment is at 10!" I yelled from upstairs. I gathered the rest of my things and started heading downstairs. "Jim!" I yelled again. Still no answer. I got downstairs to see Jim sitting in his recliner with no intentions to go anywhere.

'I'm not going to no appointment," Brenda. "Ain't nothing wrong with me."

"Jim, stop this nonsense and let's go!" I demanded.

Jim didn't budge; instead, he looked at me with his big brown eyes and motioned for me to sit on his lap. I followed Jim's instructions, and when I sat, I knew my life was about to change forever.

I sat on Jim's lap and rested my head on his head as he proceeded to tell me that he had already been to the doctor, and he knew what was wrong. Jim had been diagnosed with stage 4 lung cancer, and it was too far along for treatment. He continued to tell me that he didn't want me or the kids worrying. He lived a good life, and he wanted to spend the remainder of it doing what he loved. So when it was time for him to go, he'd go happily.

Jim and I always respected each other's wishes, and he asked that this situation be no different. "Treat me with the same love, dignity, and respect that you always have!" Jim concluded.

"I knew you were sick, Jim. I just did know it was this bad. How long have you known, Jim? And why haven't you told me?" I asked.

"Oh! But, my dear, it's not bad. I'm not in any pain," Jim assured me. I knew that wasn't the truth, but I knew he wanted me to believe that. I remained on his lap. Holding him closely. Wondering how much longer I would have this opportunity, as Jim continued.

"I've known for about 4 months. I didn't want you to worry. I don't want the kids to worry, and I certainly don't want anyone treating me differently. I'm still your husband, a father, pawpaw, and brother, and I want to be treated as such."

"We should tell the children," I mentioned.

"Absolutely not!" Jim responded. "They were just here for the holidays, and everything was perfect. That's the way I want them to remember me. I don't want them to see me as weak and fragile. I want to be remembered, as they've always known me, strong and fearless," Jim concluded.

I sat on Jim's lap until he could no longer bear my weight. That was when I decided it was time to retire. I didn't know how much time I had left with Jim, but I knew I wanted to spend it by his side.

The next morning, I submitted my retirement package and took a leave of absence while I waited for the package to be approved.

Jim was getting weaker by the day, and I knew our time was running out. It hurt me to keep this news from everyone. It was a lot to bear on my own. Jim finally agreed that I could share it with Sally.

Sally had just lost Bill a year earlier to stomach cancer. She understood exactly what I was going through. I would talk to her at night after keeping watch on Jim all day. My talks with Sally were comforting, but also devastating. Sally knew the signs all too well, and she knew my time with Jim was coming to an end, quicker than I thought. Sally urged me to invite the kids up for the upcoming MLK weekend, to give them an opportunity to say goodbye. But Jim had been so adamant about them not knowing.

I was torn against going against Jim's wishes and giving the kids the opportunity to say goodbye in person. I had never gone against anything Jim and I agreed on, but I felt so strongly about this. Against my better judgment, I asked Jim if it was OK for me to invite the kids up for the long holiday.

Jim looked at me and smiled. "Yea, I think that'll be alright. Just don't tell them I'm sick," he said. I was so surprised and happy Jim agreed.

I called the kids, not knowing if they had plans or not, but I invited them up anyway. Both boys, now men, but I've always called them my boys, were surprised by the call.

They said they had never been "invited" to come home before, and they found it hilarious, but thankfully, they agreed.

Sally decided to come up, too, for the long weekend, and I was elated.

Friday arrived, and I was overjoyed. The boys arrived Friday evening within minutes of each other and just in time to see Lace off. Lace picked Sally up from the airport for me and had plans to spend the weekend in VA. She dropped Sally off and said her goodbyes before getting on the road.

Lace still didn't know that Jim was sick. Well, we hadn't told her. I thought she knew, though. She had become extremely catering and attentive the weaker Jim became. If she did know, she surely didn't mention it.

At some point, during the weekend, the boys realized it was their opportunity to say goodbye to their father. It was heartbreaking. As Jim had instructed, I made sure everyone treated him the same and no special treatment was allowed. But it was the hardest thing to do and even harder to watch.

Overall, the weekend was great: Jim, the boys, and the grandkids had a great time. Watching them together made me realize that Jim had made the best decision for him, and I was thankful that I followed his wishes and respected his decision.

The boys lingered a little longer than they normally would on the day of their return trip. Normally, they would want to be on the road no later than ten a.m. but this time, they didn't leave until well after five p.m.

Sally decided to stay a few extra days, and I was grateful for the company. We saw the boys off, had a late supper, and Sally and I headed for bed. As always, when Lace was out of town, Jim stayed up until she got home. "She called around 6 and said she was on her way. If it's no traffic, she should make it back around 9," Jim explained. "I'll be up to bed once she gets back," he continued.

It was already close to nine. I contemplated staying up with Jim, but I knew Lace. Unless she called from the car and told you she's on the road, no telling when she'd leave. And I was exhausted, mentally and physically.

Instead, I headed upstairs to shower and get ready for bed. As I exited the shower, I heard the door, and I heard T, so I knew Lace had made it back safely. I lay down and expected Jim to be up shortly as I drifted off to sleep.

The next morning, I awoke, and Jim was gone. He passed peacefully in his sleep still sitting in his recliner.

I was so thankful that Jim had the opportunity to say goodbye to everyone he loved and everyone that loved him.

Sally came downstairs shortly after me. She didn't say anything. She allowed me to sit on Jim's lap one last time as I held him closely to me.

I saw Sally staring at me in silence, waiting for me to break so she could catch me when I fell. "You knew, didn't you? That's why you stayed?" I asked.

Sally simply responded, "I knew you needed me, that's why I stayed."

EPILOGUE

#MLK Weekend 2003

Lace and I stood there giving our statements. While they rolled Axel's body out of the house on a gurney. I stood there, far longer than I should have when I felt Lace grab my arm and ushered me inside. As we walked to go back inside, the cop entered behind us, this time without his partner. "I'm Josh's cousin. I left something here for you the night Josh got arrested," the cop said. "I'll be back after my shift to pick it up," he continued as he handed me his card.

I didn't say a word. I couldn't. I just looked at him through swollen eyes as tears began to form. Lace hissed at the cop, "Whatever the fuck you're talking about, now is not the time. Get the fuck outta her face!" Lace yelled. The cop smiled and walked off as he waved Lace away.

Lace ushered me to the sofa. She sat next to me and held me tightly. The tighter she held, the more I cried. "He was just alive this morning. And now because of me, he's dead. I shouldn't have left him!" I cried. Lace didn't respond. She just held me quietly.

Within minutes, I was immersed in multiple arms. It was Sasha and Nika. They had arrived just in time for guilt to overtake me and a range of emotions to flow out through my screams.

Axel had never done drugs before, and I couldn't understand why he would try something he had never done. What was he thinking? Was it me? Was he trying to see why I couldn't stop? All these questions rushed in and out of my thoughts repeatedly as I screamed and cried. I just couldn't understand. I would never understand.

I stayed on the couch as Sasha, Lace, and Nika each took turns holding me. The house was eerily quiet. No one said a word for hours. It was the weirdest moment I had ever experienced. Even the kids were silent. Or maybe no one was quiet, and I just couldn't process the sound of voices and noise.

I saw the movement through, and there was a lot of it, especially when the cop came back as promised. He walked in and just walked through the house like he owned the place. I saw Nika and Lace follow closely behind. He finally reemerged from my bedroom with the black duffle bag. He stood in front of me saying something, but I couldn't process it. He dipped his hand into the bag and attempted to hand me some cash. Sasha, sitting next to me, snatched it and threw it across the room. Then Sasha stood up and joined in the conversation that seemed more like an argument. I believe they were trying to figure out what was going on, but I just sat there. I didn't engage. The cop said something, forcefully, I assumed by the look on Lace's and Sasha's faces as he walked out the door.

Sasha, Lace, and Nika stared at one another and then back at me. I looked at each of them as I laid my head on the sofa. As I dozed off, I couldn't help but think, "I'll never forgive myself. If only I had kept my promise to get rid of the bag, Axel would have never been tempted to try drugs. He would have never overdosed, and he wouldn't be dead."

www.ingramcontent.com/pod-product-compliance
Lightning Source LLC
Chambersburg PA
CBHW050819180626
46814CB00004B/1362